THE RETRIAL

OF

LILLIAN S. RAIZEN

A LIFE AVENGED

INSPIRED BY TRUE EVENTS

by

Gerri L. Schaffer

DORRANCE PUBLISHING CO
EST. 1920
PITTSBURGH, PENNSYLVANIA 15238

Dorrance Publishing Co
585 Alpha Drive
Suite 103
Pittsburgh, PA 15238
Visit our website at *www.dorrancebookstore.com*

ISBN: 978-1-6853-7146-3
eISBN: 978-1-6853-7989-6

Unfortunately, I never met my great-aunt Lillian, as my family never acknowledged her existence. In 1970, the year she died, I was twenty-two years old. Perhaps I wasn't ready to process the full meaning of her motives or understand the circumstances surrounding them, and thus could not do justice in putting this sensational story to print. But, oh, how I wish time could be reversed! I would look into her eyes with unspoken empathy and understanding, and then gently embrace her with welcoming arms.

This book is dedicated to
my daughter, grandchildren
and the Schaffer family,
whose indomitable spirits will
reverberate throughout eternity.

ACKNOWLEDGMENTS

First and foremost, I wish to thank my daughter, Heather. She was the original cheerleader for this project, and her unwavering support kept me going through all of life's hurdles. I also wish to acknowledge friend and colleague, Susan Fineo, who orchestrated permission to retrieve the illusive Trial Transcript at the New York Bar Association Library, spent countless hours researching a file number that was necessary to attain the case of appeal, and subsequently helping me to copy the 1,000 page trial transcript in the early 1990s when copiers were practically just invented! My cousins Alan and Annette Geiss, both avid readers and members of Net Galley, Good Reads, and the AMA, were also great morale boosters, editors and in addition, medical and legal advisors. Much appreciation to Richard Schaffer, our family archivist, who supplied precious primary resources and to Stewart Schaffer, my brother, for his technical advice and for giving me the impetus to remain true to my vision. A nod goes to Vicki Kirschbaum who was one of the earliest researchers, helping me to locate all the newspaper articles of that era, before there were smart phones and the internet.

Recent sources and people I consider true friends include Marge Harrison, a colleague, dear friend and a brilliant mind, who spent many breakfasts parlaying ideas and offering her keen insight into different aspects of the psychological angles greatly needed to understand the motives of those involved in the case. Marilyn Gotkin, whose passion is genealogy, uncovered articles and pictures of Lillian and other information which added to this work.

A most important person, Liz Ropers, dear friend, colleague, confidante and literary consultant, has been an unbelievable sounding board, editor, mentor and critic for days and months on end. She has walked and talked me through some difficult decisions when we couldn't wrap our brains around the 'whys and wherefores'. Her invaluable time, input and wisdom have helped me to finally put this book forward.

I will be forever grateful to all with whom I have collaborated, and I am eternally grateful to the many people who have encouraged me along the way, supplied me with information and given me insight and determination to write my great-aunt Lillian's story, to my dearest friends who were brilliant resources themselves and finally to my family whom I love with all my heart.

List of Characters

Lawyers
Benjamin Reass-defense attorney
Albert Conway-defense attorney
Joseph V. Gallagher-prosecuting attorney

The Schaffers
Lillian S. Raizen-defendant
Sadie Schaffer-one of Lillian's six sisters
Jacob Schaffer

Friends of the Schaffer Family
Dr. Abraham Glickstein-family physician and
close friend of patriarch, Jacob Schaffer (father of Lillian)
Charles Raizen-boyhood sweetheart and husband of Lillian
Minnie Tulipan-neighbor and acquaintance of Lillian

Passengers on Boat to Savannah
Charles Robbins
Mary Robbins-mother of Charles Robbins

Raymond Street Jail
Harry C. Honeck-Warden
Dr. Stetzer-visiting physician

Daytona Florida-Orange Villa Hotel
Helen Weber-guest

Passengers on Boat from Savannah to New York
Robert Swayne Perry
Isaac Cohen
Levern Boardwell

Miscellaneous
Albert Bradley-bus boy and acquaintance of Lillian
Dr. Buchhalter-friend of Glickstein

Alienists (old term meaning psychologist or psychiatrist)
George H. Kirby
Edward E. Hicks
Charles W. Pilgram
Isham G. Harris

Jurors

1. William P. Callaghan
2. Henry J. McAteer
3. William Darbee
4. Phineas B. Blanchard
5. Charles L. Huisking
6. Edward G. McGrover
7. Theordore T. Hendrickson
8. Elmer E. Day
9. Harold C. Kinsey
10. Samuel L. Greason
11. Samuel M. Moneypenny
12. Everett S. Swalm

PROLOGUE

Revenge is an act of passion; vengeance of justice. Injuries are revenged; crimes are avenged. Samuel Johnson

1946

As I looked into the chapel from the now closed double doors, I realized, at that very moment, how often I was the one who was always on the outside looking in, on the rim of life, never really having one to call my own. My family was now seated and the bride and groom ready to take their vows. How lovely they both looked and how in love they seemed to be. Not to be included in this family affair was actually customary and normal for me. I loved my nephew, Howard, and how I wished him a full rewarding life....one I haven't known and most assuredly will never know!

Standing there atop the St. George hotel, I felt small, obsequious. This grand hotel was a magnet for the rich and famous. The sheer magnitude of its one-block occupancy, had a thirty-story tower, the biggest and grandest of the time. F. Scott Fitzgerald tipped a glass here and Presidents Truman and Roosevelt graced its rooms. Truman Capote swam the largest salt water Olympic size pool in the United States. My mind flashed to the one and only time, like Alice who ate the mushrooms, that I became supernatural and large, my head hitting the ceiling, and it all came back to me, once again, as it always did.

Growing up in Brooklyn was blithe and unfettered. The second-born child of Jacob and Anna Schaffer, I was one of six children who frolicked the streets of Flatbush in Brooklyn, New York. My siblings and I adored playing games in the street, like stoopball, marbles and skully. We would tear down the street to the nearest park to cool off in the summertime. The cobblestones were cold and refreshing on the soles of my feet. We would spend many hours there being fancy-free. I could breathe then.

I can't remember any incident with a dog or a cat that instilled the fear of God in me, but I did have an irrational fear when one was nearby. If I was walking with one of my sisters and a dog came along, I would scream bloody murder until she chased the animal away.

By Mr. Conway

Testimony by Sadie Schaffer (the defendant's sister)

Q. During the years as they went along, is there anything that you can tell us about your observations of your sister with reference to cats or dogs? A. Yes, she was very much afraid of cats and dogs, to this extent, that if she ever met—coming home from business, I will say, she would see a cat or a dog in her way, she would go across the street and yell and try to attract our attention as best she could. Sometimes, perhaps on a cold day when all the windows were shut, would run around the corner and telephone.

Q. Telephone to what? A. To tell us to chase the cat or dog, which ever it was, away.

Q. Did that happen on more than one occasion? A. Oh yes, a number of occasions.

This childhood fear manifested itself after my first few visits with Dr. Glickstein, our family doctor and a good friend of my father.

Minnie A. Tulipan, 1922 Avenue M, Borough of Brooklyn, City of New York, a witness called on behalf of the defendant, having been first duly sworn, testified as follows:

Direct Examination by Mr. Conway:

Q. How long have you known Mrs. Raizen, please, Mrs. Tulipan? A. About fifteen years.

Q. During part of that time did you know her intimately? A. Very.

Q. During which portion of the fifteen years was that? The first part or the second part? A. The first part.

Q. Can you tell us between what years that was, please? A. About 1909 to 1914 or 1915.

Q. And did you observe Mrs. Raizen during that time, during that period of intimacy? A. Yes.

Q. Did you notice anything with reference to her actions or her talk that impressed you? Just yes or no. A. I did.

Q. Madam? A. Yes.

Q. Will you please state what you observed? A. Well, she was very temperamental at all times.

Q. What? A. Temperamental.

Q. What did you notice that made you say that? A. Her feelings would play upon her at different times.

Q. How? A. She would be very happy at one moment and very sad the next—gloomy, crying. She liked to play the piano and sing and then stop.

Q. Stop when? A. In the midst of singing.

Q. When you say crying, what did you notice with reference to her crying? A. Hysterically crying.

Q. How often during a given period would you see her do that? How often during a month? A. There were certain times of the month that I would notice it more than others.

Q. How many times during the month did you notice, please? A. That is kind of hard to answer.

Q. One or two or— A. Probably one or two.

Q. What else did you observe about her, please, Mrs. Tulipan? A. Well, will you be more explicit?

Q. Did you ever notice anything about her conduct? What about biting her nails? A. Oh, yes, very often she would bite her nails and crack her knuckles and bite her lips always. I would call her down for it.

Q. When you say very often, what do you mean by that? A. Well, she became agitated sometimes over very little.

Q. What for instance? A. Why, just a little argument as girl-friends would have.

Q. What would the agitation be? What did she do? A. As I say, she would bite her lips and crack her knuckles, as we would say, and bite her nails.

Q. Crack her knuckles by pulling them out? A. Doing this (indication).

Q. Was she nervous? A. Very.

Q. All the time you knew her? A. Yes.

Q. Can you say whether she was worrisome or not? A. Pardon me?

Q. Can you say whether she was worrisome or not? A. Oh, very worrisome sometimes over trifles.

Q. What did you see her do that made you say she was worrisome? A. Just what I have explained now. That is what makes me know that she was very worrisome. Any little argument at home would immediately bring these things on.

Q. Were you at her wedding? A. Yes.

Q. Did you observe her appearance that night? A. Yes, indeed.

Q. What did you notice or observe about her appearance on that night? A. It broke my heart to see her as thin as she was.

Q. As what? A. As thin as she was.

Q. Had she been stouter? A. Very much stouter.

Q. Can you tell us about how much weight you think she lost? A. Oh, I should judge fifty to sixty pounds.

Q. Did you speak to her about it on the night of her wedding? A. I did. We danced together and I said, "Lillian, why are you so thin and why do you look so badly? This is not the night for it."

She said, "Minnie, if I could only tell you. My mother is before me, but I can't tell anything." At the time I didn't know what it meant. I thought it was because her mother had died.

Q. Don't tell what you thought, please. Did you see her after her marriage at any time? A. Yes, once. We visited them.

Q. Did you observe anything with reference to her physical condition at that time? A. Just the same as the wedding night. Very thin and nervous.

Q. What did you ever observe, if anything with reference to animals in connection with Mrs. Raizen? A. She would be dreadfully afraid of dogs. If she would see them, she would grab my arm— "Minnie, there is a dog coming," and she would cry, and I would laugh, thinking that it was very funny.

Mr. Conway: You may examine.

Cross-Examination by Mr. Gallagher:

Q. Do you know when her mother died? A. Not exactly, but several months prior to her wedding.

Q. Around Christmas, wasn't it, 1920? A. Probably. I don't remember the date.

Q. You know that family very well, don't you? A. Very well.

Q. Did you attend the funeral of the mother? A. No, I didn't. I was sick at the time.

Q. That was five or six months before her wedding? A. Yes, I believe it was.

Q. On the night of the wedding she told you that her mother was before her, didn't she? A. Yes.

Q. Are there any animals that you are afraid of? A. Lions.

Q. Are you afraid of mice? A. Why, no.

Q. Not at all? A. No.

Q. Did you ever talk to Mrs. Raizen, then Miss Schaffer, about reducing her weight? A. No.

Q. Did you ever hear her say that she took a course in weight reduction? A. No, I did not.

Q. You don't know anything about it? A. No.

Friends

My father and Abraham Glickstein were friends. Our families were intertwined in my early years and I shared many play days with his daughters. As I matured and had five siblings of my own, I gradually lost touch with those girls and took on responsibilities to help my mother. From 1900-1912 I had intermittent doctor visits for various ailments in my youth. Mother always came along, but the doctor always examined me in another room, privately. He was always overly attentive, and I recall one specific time that his hands made me feel very uncomfortable. He would ask me about my singing and interests while brushing his hands across my developing breasts and pre-pubic lower area. He had this habit of touching himself in a way that was confusing to me; rubbing his crotch in a jerky fashion. As a young child, I just accepted this again and again, adding each unpleasant experience to a shelf in my mind. To me, he was bigger than life. As I adored my father, and the doctor was his friend, I buried his actions deep in my mind and became infatuated with the idea that the doctor was actually interested in my life. I became overly impressed with successful people in business, and my own interests drifted in that direction. I recall the many hours spent with Pop, always immersed in heavy conversation about tin manufacturing, marketing and profits. He had a tin company and was known as "The Tin King" of Brooklyn. I felt an element of pride being the 'Tin King's Daughter'.

As I became a young woman, I came down with what was called then as the grippe. Today it would probably be diagnosed as the flu or some other virus. My symptoms were classic: sore throat, congestion and aches and pains. My mother insisted that I see the doctor. Hesitant to do so, for some inexplicable reason at that time, I always obliged my mother.

When I arrived at the doctor's house, I went through the living area, first, to give my greetings to the family. That is when I sat down at the piano and started to play and sing. I didn't realize that the doctor had come into the room and was staring at me. After I ended my song, he asked me to come into his office. He complimented my voice, asked about my family and complimented me again, saying that he always knew that I would grow into a fine girl. Although I was there for treatment of the grippe, my mother explained to him, in a prior conversation, that I had another, more personal woman's issue that needed to be addressed. I expressed my concern over frequent menstruation and profuse discharge prior to its onset. He gave me medication for my grippe and orders to stay in bed for a couple of weeks. I was to see him when I felt better to address the other problem. He was emphatic that it needed to be 'looked into'.

ESTABLISHED 1888

MANUFACTURERS AND JOBBERS

*Nearly Forty Years of
a Progressive
Industry*

THE SCHAFFER TINWARE MFG. CO.
76-86 Sedgwick Street
Brooklyn, N. Y.
Phone HENry ★ 0369

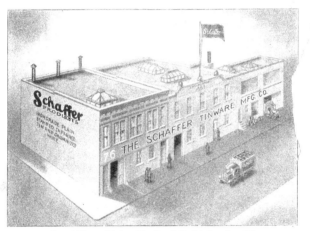

General Offices and Factory at Brooklyn, N. Y.   Telephone Henry 0369

The Schaffer Organization

The reputation for quality and constructive industrial policy of The Schaffer Tinware Manufacturing Company is back of every piece of Schaffer Products. All materials used in the manufacture of Schaffer Products are of the best to be obtainable. Your complete satisfaction is assured.

In presenting this, our latest catalogue, we respectfully call your particular attention to the various patented articles, which are distinctive and exclusively "SCHAFFER PRODUCTS" and are designed exclusively by us.

An enviable business reputation, developed during the many years of successful manufacturing and merchandising, is responsible for the high standard of SCHAFFER quality and workmanship, and of which we are justly proud.

The constant increasing demand for "SCHAFFER PRODUCTS," by new and old friends, has given us the substantial foundation for continued success.

We are always striving to make the words SCHAFFER and HIGHEST QUALITY synonomous. This permits unqualified endorsements for *highest quality* and *healthful purposes* of Schaffer Products by Health Officials, Pure Food Experts and Good Housekeepers.

Yours sincerely,

THE SCHAFFER TINWARE MANUFACTURING COMPANY

ROLL TOP BREAD AND CAKE BOXES
WITH DRAWER

Extra Heavy Enamel Ware
Handsomely Japanned in Assorted Colors
Decalcomania Decorations
Packed in Individual Cartons

Numbers	1	1½	2
Length, inches	13¼	16	....
Width, inches	10⅝	11½	....
Height, inches	10⅝	11½	....
White, per dozen	....	....	....
Blue, per dozen	....	....	....
French Grey, per dozen	....	....	....

W R I T E   F O R   L A T E S T   P R I C E   Q U O T A T I O N S

DOCTOR CONVICTED AND ARRESTED FOR DRUG TRAFFICKING

ARREST PHYSICIAN AFTER OPIUM RAID

Dr. N. Glickstein Held in $5,000 Bail for Illegal Traffic in the Drug.

SEE BIG SMUGGLING PLOT

Customs Man Finds Chinaman Laden with Thirty-Pound Package —Three Others Held.

Dr. Nathan Glickstein of 218 Henry Street, his brother, Elias Glickstein; Isidore Goldstein, and Nathan Ulrich were arraigned yesterday in the Federal District Court before Commissioner Shields on a complaint made by Customs Inspector Walter P. Murphy, charging that they were engaged in a conspiracy with Lee Sing, a Chinaman living in Brooklyn, to violate the laws of the United States by manufacturing opium for smoking purposes. The Commissioner held Dr. Glickstein and Ulrich in $5,000 bail each, Goldstein in $1,000 bail, and Elias Glickstein in $500 bail for examination on Feb. 7.

The discovery of what Gen. Nelson Henry, the Surveyor of the Port, believes to be a big opium smuggling scheme was made by Inspector Murphy on Saturday afternoon at the Brooklyn entrance to the Brooklyn Bridge, when he noticed Lee Sing carrying a bundle in a suspicious manner and arrested him. He is now in the Raymond Street Jail. When it was opened the package was found to contain thirty pounds of crude opium, which the Chinaman said he had purchased from Einer & Amen, wholesale chemists, Third Avenue and Eighteenth Street, on a prescription from Dr. Glickstein. When the Inspector went to the chemist he was told by a salesman named Cahill that two five-pound packages had been purchased the same morning on Dr. Glickstein's order, and in addition he had sent for quantities of cocaine in September, October, and November until the head of the firm issued orders that Glickstein was not to be supplied with cocaine.

When Inspector Murphy went to Dr. Glickstein's office on Wednesday afternoon after the arrest of Lee Sing the doctor was away, but Elias Glickstein was there with Goldstein and Ulrich. All three were arrested by the detectives who accompanied the Inspector. In the offices were three pounds of gum opium and some hop toi jars. The doctor's books showed that he had purchased $1,500 worth of cocaine in three months from Einer & Amen. The crude opium was sold to Chinamen by messengers, it is alleged, at $8 a pound, who reduced it into smoking opium and retailed it to their countrymen at $40 to $50. He had names of white men as well as Chinamen on his books, the Customs Inspector said.

Dr. Glickstein, who was away in New England, heard of the raid of his office and his brother's arrest and returned to New York yesterday morning. When he called at the Custom House to see the Surveyor one of Henkel's Deputy United States Marshals was waiting with a warrant for his arrest.

Gen. Henry said that he believed Dr. Glickstein was the head of an extensive opium smuggling conspiracy.

CONVICT A DRUG DEALER.

Two Years in Prison and Fine of $3,000 for East Side Physician.

Dr. Abraham Glickstein of 218 Henry Street was found guilty yesterday in the Federal District Court in this city of having used the mails in violation of the law prohibiting the sale of cocaine in the State of New York and of having engaged in the manufacture and sale of opium for smoking contrary to the Federal statutes. The case was considered important by the Government, as Glickstein, who was a licensed physician, was said to be the head of a widespread organisation for the sale of the drugs.

Judge Mayer imposed a sentence on Glickstein of two years in Atlanta prison and a fine of $3,000.

The New York Times

Published: July 4, 1913
Copyright © The New York Times

TRIAL TRANSCRIPT PAGES 411-426

Lillian S. Raizen, 814 Avenue W Borough of Brooklyn, City of New York, the defendant herein, a witness called in here on her own behalf, having been first duly sworn, testified as follows:

By Mr. Conway:

Q. Mrs. Raizen, your husband is Mr. Charles Raizen, is he not? A. Yes, sir.

Q. You knew Dr. Glickstein in his life, did you not? A. Yes, sir.

Q. How long did you know him? A. Since I was a little girl.

Q. How old were you when you first met him, if you remember? A. I don't remember. I was a small girl.

Q. I can't hear you. A. I was a small girl.

Q. Now I want the jury to hear you. So please keep up your voice just as much as you can. A. I will try, Mr. Conway.

Q. How old were you when you first knew or met Dr. Glick-stein, please? A. I don't know how old I was, but I was young.

Q. A small child? A. Yes I was little more than an infant.

Q. Where did you live then, please? A. On Madison Street.

Q. What number? A. I don't remember. I think it was 183.

Q. Did Glickstein at that time live in the same house with you, if you remember. A. Yes.

Q. On what floor did you live? A. Upstairs.

Q. You lived there with your father and mother and sisters and brother, did you? A. Yes.

Q. Do you remember when it was that you were first treated by Dr. Glickstein for any ailment? A. All the time.

Q. Do you remember an occasion in 1915 or 1916 where you went to him to be treated for grippe? A. I do.

Q. Do you remember what part of the year it was, or don't you? A. Either in the spring or fall, Mr. Conway.

Q. Did you go to his place? A. I did.

Q. His office? A. I did.

Q. Where was his office at that time, if you remember? A. I think it was on South Fifth Street—I think.

Q. In Brooklyn? A. In Brooklyn.

Q. Do you know the number? A. I do not.

Q. Where did you work at that time, please? A. At Alexander & Company.

Q. You were working for Mr. Alexander, who was on the

stand here day before yesterday? A. Yes, sir; yes, sir.

Q. When you reached the Doctor's office that day was he there or did you have to wait for him? A. I came there in the afternoon, the middle of the afternoon, and I had to wait. I had to wait.

Q. Did you do anything while waiting? A. Yes, sir.

Q. What was that? A. I played the piano.

Q. What? A. I played the piano.

Q. You knew his family, did you not? A. Very well. Yes, yes, yes.

Q. Now, while you were playing the piano, did any one come in? A. Yes, but I didn't hear it.

Q. Who was that? A. The Doctor.

Q. Did you have some conversation with him at that time? A. I did.

Q. What was the conversation, please? A. I didn't hear him come in.

Q. Yes? A. And he stood for a long while, and I heard something in the room and I turned and I saw him there and I was embarrassed; and he says, "I am sorry," he says, "that you heard me. That singing was beautiful. Play some more and sing some more." I felt—

Q. What happened after that, please? A. He treated me.

Q. What did you tell him was the matter with you at that time? A. I told him that I was suffering with a cold and that it seemed to be in my entire body and I couldn't get rid of it, and I wanted him to look me over and treat me for it.

Q. Did he ask you any questions on that occasion, or was that about the substance of it? A. He gave me some prescriptions. He told me to go home and stay in bed for a couple of weeks and—that is all.

Q. And what? A. And that is all.

Q. Well, now, did you go home? A. I did.

Q. And did you stay home the following day? A. Oh, he asked me something else.

Q. What was that, please? A. He asked me about the family.

Q. What, please? A. My family, my whole family.

Q. Yes? A. And my mother and father and how they were feeling.

Q. Yes? A. And I said that they were all right, and he said— he spoke to me a long time. He hadn't seen me for a long time. He says I had grown very nicely. He says he always knew that I would grow up to be a very fine girl and I didn't disappoint him, but he says he never knew that I had such a charming voice. He asked me about my general health.

Q. Yes? A. And I told him I was ashamed to tell him and he noticed I was ashamed, and then he urged me to speak, and I spoke, and I told him that—oh, he asked me—he asked me first—he says, "How is your menstruation?" I says to him, "That is just what I wanted to ask you about, Doctor."

He says, "I knew. What is it?" I says—I said to him—I says, "Doctor,"

I says, "I menstruate very frequently, and the flow is very scant, and prior to my periods of menstruation I suffer with a profuse discharge."

He says, "That is quite serious, Lillian. You should have that looked into immediately," but he says, "You have got to cure your grippe first."

Q. Cure what first? A. My grippe. He says, "Go home and go to bed and get cured of the grippe, but don't neglect," he says, "the other matter."

Q. "Don't neglect the other matter"? A. Yes, he says, "It needs to be looked into."

Q. Did you stay home the next day, if you recall? A. No, I didn't stay home, because Mr. Alexander called up and he spoke to my mother. He asked my mother if I could come to the office—that there was something that needed my attention.

Q. You went, did you? A. Into the office.

Q. While you were at the office, did you receive a telephone call from anybody? A. Yes, yes, Mr. Conway.

Q. From whom was that, please? A. It was from the Doctor.

Q. That was about how long after you reached the office, please? A. Quite soon after.

Q. And what did he say to you? A. He censured me for going to the office. He says he had given me medicine that didn't permit me to expose my body to the air, and that I should not have gone to the office. He said that he called up my mother to ask of my condition and my mother told him that I went to the office and he says, "What a fool! Give me her number. I will call her up and tell her to go right home."

Q. He did, did he? He did call you up? A. Yes, but I told him—

Q. What else did he say? A. I told the Doctor—I said, "It is very kind of you to take such an interest in me, but I am feeling so sick I intended to leave in a minute anyway," and I said to him—I says to him, "I intended to leave in a minute." Oh, yes, but that I had to go to the office; there were some notes to be paid and I had to pay them. That is all Mr. Conway.

Q. When did you next see Dr. Glickstein? A. I saw him, you know, right after my next menstrual period.

Q. About how long after, please? A. Not very long after. Just a few weeks.

Q. You went to his office to see him, did you? A. I did. Oh, when I came home, I spoke of it to mother, and mother says to me, "The Doctor called up and he said, 'How is the prima donna?'" And mother says—

Q. I don't think that is important. A. All right, Mr. Conway.

Q. I want to keep within the rules. You went back, you say, some little time later, did you? A. Yes.

Q. What occurred then, please? Did you have some further talk with him? A. Yes.

Q. What was it about, please? Just tell us in your own way. A. He talked and talked and talked to me.

Q. What about? A. About everything imaginable. Everything imaginable.

Q. Well, about what? A. About himself, about his family, about my family—

Q. Yes? A. About me, about what I was doing, about what I intended to do with singing—

Q. Yes? A. About—oh, about everything. About everything.

Q. Were you treated on that day by him? A. Yes, he treated me, Mr. Conway.

Q. For what? A. He said in words that I didn't understand I didn't understand—he used some Latin phrases, but I gathered from what he said that it was necessary for me to receive such treatment as would stretch some part of my organs—I don't know—only that my menstruation should come better and then I wouldn't get the discharge and I would become much healthier; and he did. He did.

Q. Yes? What else did he say, please, if anything? A. Oh, he says lots of things. What do you want to know? Just what?

Q. Was that about all that was said on that topic, please? A. That I remember just this minute.

Q. Did you receive any treatment? A. I did, Mr. Conway.

Q. On that— A. I did. I did.

Q. On that day? A. Yes, I think—no, I don't know if it was that day or whether he says come back with mother, I don't know just what it was—whether it was on that day or the next trip. But he said for me—oh, he said that a course of treatments would be necessary. That is what he told me. That is just what he told me—a course of treatment would be necessary, and I told mama about it. She says, "All right, whatever, the doctor says," Yes, this is right.

Q. On that day or thereafter did you receive certain treatments for this condition? A. I did, Mr. Conway.

Q. What did that treatment consist in? A. I don't know, but it caused me pain. I don't know what treatment it was. I don't know.

Q. You were treated vaginally, were you? A. I was, Mr. Conway, I was.

Q. Where were you when you were treated? A. On the table, whatever it is.

Q. When you say a table, do you mean a doctor's table? A. Yes, sir, I call it a doctor's table, yes.

Q. I show you this photograph that has been marked People's Exhibit Six, and I ask you if you see in this photograph a table such as you have referred to in your testimony just now. A. (The witness rocked her body back and forth with her hands against her face.)

The Court: Look at the picture, please. (After a pause) Take it away. She will not look at it.

The Witness: I didn't know what you were doing. I didn't know what you were doing.

Q. Mrs. Raizen, how many treatments did you receive on this table before anything occurred between you and the Doctor? A. A few. I couldn't tell you if it was one. I couldn't tell you if it was two, but it was a few.

Q. After a few of those treatments of which you have told us, did something occur? A. Yes, sir.

Q. What was that, please? A. Do you mean when the Doctor attacked me, Mr. Conway?

Q. Yes. A. Yes, he attacked me. I was lying on the table.

Q. When you lay on this table, were you lying on your back or on your side or how? A. Yes, sir, on my back. On my back.

Q. Where were your feet, Mrs. Raizen? A. In the stirrups. My heels were in the stirrups.

Q. Will you look at this picture, Exhibit Six, and see whether you see in that picture something—

A. Could you spare me that, Mr. Conway? Could you?

Q. Well, all right. A. Could you? I wish you would.

Q. All right. A. I wish you would.

Q. You said that the Doctor attacked you. Do you mean that he forcibly— A. I mean what I said, that he attacked me.

Q. After that had happened, will you just tell what happened that day, please? A. Yes, I can tell you. I can tell you.

Q. Yes. A. I found it hard to rise. I was stunned. I was petrified and I tried to raise my body. I finally did. I stood and I stared and I finally found him at the other end of the room, and as I looked at him, he was tearing his shirt off him and he was changing his shirt.

Q. Yes? A. I looked down at myself, and I says, "Oh, Doctor, look! Look at this!" He said, "That is nothing," he said, "Lillian, your menses dropped." I didn't know what menses was. I didn't know what it meant, and I commenced to cry, and he tried to console me. He tried, but it was hard. I think he took me home. Oh, he took his shirt and changed it and he rolled it up and he put it in his outside pocket. I saw that.

Q. You did go home, you say? A. Yes, I got home.

Q. What did you do, please, after you got home? A. I think he took me home. I don't remember. I think he took me home.

Q. What did you do that night, if anything? A. I sat up. He gave me—he gave me a towel with which to protect myself, and I sat up. I sat up. I don't think I went to bed. I sat up.

Q. You say you sat up that night? Do you remember what happened the next day or what condition you were in the next day, please? A. Yes, I was in very bad condition, Mr. Conway.

Q. In what way, please? A. I was in very bad condition, Mr. Conway.

Q. In what way, please? A. I was stupefied. I don't know—I was stupefied. I went to the office and tried to work, and I couldn't work. I tried to think and it was hard for me to think. I had respected him. I couldn't understand. I was beside myself.

Q. Did you hear from the Doctor that day? A. Yes, yes he called me up several times.

Q. Did you speak to him or he to you on the wire? A. I did, I did, Mr. Conway.

Q. What was said? Do you remember? A. Oh, he tried to talk to me. I couldn't talk. I couldn't speak. He says to me, "Lillian, I want you to come down to the office this evening. I want to talk to you. Don't cry." And I went down. I went to the office.

Q. What happened then? A. Nothing. I just sat there, Mr. Conway. I stayed there, that is all. He used to show me all the different things he was doing—bandages he was making and the treatment he was giving different patients, prior to this attack, and I interested myself very much in medicine and he told me I was a wonderful girl, that bookkeeping was beneath my attainments and that I should try medicine. He thought I would make a wonderful medical woman, and I was flattered. I thought that I didn't understand my own value and that I could study medicine. He said he would give me the practice right in his office, because there weren't—well, I don't like to say this. He said that his people were not sufficiently interested in him to assist him, and that if I assisted him, I would take care of his office and take care of his patients and keep his telephone, and I would gain my own practice and then of course I would be known as Dr. Lillian Schaffer.

Q. Were these things told to you before this day of the attack?

A. Yes, sir, Mr. Conway, yes.

Q. On the day following this attack of which you have told us, you say you went and sat there and that he spoke to you?

A. He tried to speak to me. He tried to show me the different things in his office, but I just sat and I stared at him. It was all different to me. I was different.

Q. Did you want to go there that night? A. I just went. I didn't know what I wanted to do, so I went.

Q. Did you hear from the Doctor after that? A. Yes, I heard from him regularly.

Q. How often? A. Oh, a few times every single day.

Q. A few times what, please? A. Every single day.

Q. Was that by telephone? A. By telephone, Mr. Conway.

Q. Did he ask you to do certain things? A. Always asked— he asked me everything. He asked me about my menstruation. He treated me after that, too. I went there for treatments after that.

Q. A short time after this attack did you go to him and tell him anything about your condition as to sleepiness, or did he ask you anything about your condition? A. He asked me everything. I told him everything. He asked me everything.

Q. Within some little time after that did he ask you about your condition and did you tell him that you were very sleepy and drowsy? A. Yes, he asked me if I had menstruated, and I told him. I told him I had not menstruated. He said, "How do you feel?" I said, "I feel very, very sleepy. I can't keep my eyes open."

Q. What happened then? A. Then he told me to meet him at a certain place.

Q. Do you remember where the place was? A. He told me to meet him. I met him and he took me up somewhere on the east side of Harlem to a man's house.

Q. Do you remember about what street it was on? A. In the neighborhood of 100th Street on the east side of Harlem.

Q. About how long was that after this? A. I couldn't tell you, Mr. Conway. It was a matter of months, but I couldn't tell you just when.

Q. What happened there, please? A. There was a man. He says to him, "How do you do, Mr. Efron?" The man was standing, I remember, in the kitchen.

Q. Eftron? A. Efron, yes, Efron.

Q. Yes? A. And he took me in there. I was scared. I thought he was taking me to you know—a place that was not nice, but it was a nice place. It was a nice residence. The people appeared respectable, and he took me in there. I had a feeling of what he was going to do, but I didn't know exactly. I thought he was going to take me there and give me a strong dose of medicine, and I knew that it was menstruation that he wanted to bring on, and I thought he was going to give me a strong dose of medicine and watch me, I suppose, until the menstruation would come. But instead he took off his overcoat, he took off his suit coat, and he rolled up his sleeves, and he seemed to be very familiar with the place. He took a kitchen table and placed it in the living room. The people of the house—they owned the house but they didn't notice it. He went about as though he knew the place, and he put the table in the center of the room, and I grew very frightened, and then he gave me something to drink. He saw that I was growing very hysterical, and he said, "Calm yourself." I said, "What are you going to do?" He said, "You mind your business and keep quiet. Leave that entirely to me." I kept quiet.

Q. Then what happened? A. And then he got some sheets and he got medicines.

Q. Did you see anybody else there, Mrs. Raizen? A. And he prepared an improvised operating room, and I grew very frightened. He told me to remove my clothes.

Q. Did you see anybody else there at any time? A. I didn't see anybody else there until he had me on the table. He strapped me to the table, and as the sheet was over me—he put a sheet over me, and someone uncovered the sheet. I don't know who it was, and I thought it was he, and I looked up and I saw someone else.

Q. Were you given an anesthetic at that time, Mrs. Raizen. A. Yes. That is the person that gave it to me. That is the person that gave it to me, the one whom I looked up at.

Q. Do you know how long you remained at that place? A. A couple of hours—I don't know—all afternoon. I don't know how long.

Q. How did you get home, if you recall? A. He took me home. He took me home.

Q. In his automobile? A. Yes, sir. He made a call to my mother when he took me home.

Q. At this time, Mrs. Raizen, at the time of this attack, you knew your present husband, did you not? A. I did, Mr. Conway.

Q. You and he had been keeping company? A. Since childhood.

Q. You had both lived over in New York together, had you not? A. Yes, sir; yes, sir; yes, sir.

Q. After these occasions, the occasion that you have mentioned of the attack and the occasion after that time when you were brought up to this house a month later— A. Yes.

Q. Did you continue to hear from Dr. Glickstein? A. All the time.

Q. When you say all the time, just what do you mean by that? A. I didn't understand your question, Mr. Conway.

Q. When you say all the time just what do you mean by that? A. Every day. All the time.

Q. Every day, you mean? A. Yes.

Q. Was that by telephone or letter? A. Strictly by telephone.

Q. On the telephone did he tell you to do certain things? A. Yes, he told me. He asked me.

Q. When I say, did he tell you to do certain things, I mean did he tell you at various times to come to his house? A. Yes, sir: yes, sir.

Q. On all of the occasions during this period when he told you to come to his house, did you ever fail to go to his house? A. I don't think so.

Q. Did you ever, after any of these telephone calls make up your mind not to go? A. No, I would sometimes very often—

Q. Did you ever, after any of these telephone calls, make up your mind not to go? A. Yes, sir.

Q. What happened then? A. And then I would go.

Q. What happened in between the time when you made up your mind not to go and the time you did? A. I would make up my mind not to go, and as the time was approaching. I would almost hear him say to me, "Eight o'clock," and I was there at 8 o'clock.

Q. This continued for how long, Mrs. Raizen? A. For several years, Mr. Conway, several years.

Q. Was there any other operations ever performed upon you besides the one you have mentioned? A. Two other operations—two others.

Q. Long after this had continued for several years, in 1918 or 1919, did you hear of Christian Science? A. Yes, sir, Mr. Conway.

Q. Where did you hear of it or how did you hear of it? A. I think at my office. I don't know just where. I think at my office.

Q. After you heard of it, what did you do? A. I went to the church.

Q. During this time, while you and your present husband were courting or while he was courting you— A. Yes.

Q. (Continuing) —and the time when this relation was continued for several years, as you stated— A. Yes.

Q. (Continuing) —did Dr. Glickstein ever talk to you about your husband? A. Yes.

Q. Or you to him? A. He talked to me about my husband on the first or second or third visit to his office, at that time, at the first or second or third—on the initial visit with that condition of grippe.

Q. Do you recall generally what was said Mrs. Raizen? A. I do. He asked me just what my sweetheart was—I don't know just what he said—is doing, and I told him; and at that time I was very curious about medicine, and knowing different things in medicine. I regarded it as something higher up, and I asked him about the condition that existed in Charlie, and he said, "Oh, what do you want to have anything to do with a fellow like that for?" Shall I tell you what I asked him?

Q. Yes, surely. A. I says to him, "You know, Doctor," I says, "Charlie has—he gets a very severe pain at times, and it is so acute that nothing allays the pain except—"

Q. Let me interrupt you. You told him, without going into these details, that Charlie had some kidney trouble? A. Yes.

Q. Which gave him pain? A. Yes.

Q. What did he say? That is what we are interested in. A. What did he say about what?

Q. When you told him that, what did he say? A. He said I should not have anything to do with a fellow like that, because it is a condition— "How many attacks do you think he can stand of that? That is a condition that is fatal, and you don't know" —I began getting cold as he was talking to me. "Oh," I says, "Doctor, but I love Charlie." He says, "That is just the trouble with all you foolish girls," and he mimicked me. He says, "I love Charlie!" But he says, "If you marry Charlie and you have a child, eventually one of these attacks will come on him," he says, "and you will lose Charlie," he says, "if you don't know of his condition before." He says, "If you do, well, that is different, but why should you go into anything with your eyes wide open?"

Q. That worried you, didn't it? A. It certainly did, Mr. Conway.

Q. And you grieved over it? A. Yes, I did.

Q. You had never talked to your present husband about what you had learned about that? A. No, I wouldn't upset Charlie.

Dr. Rebecca Housel

What is a Svengali?

'AN INCLUDES'

The 1895 novel *TRILBY* by French author, George du Maurier (1834-1896), features the character, Svengali, a psychiatrist who completely controls a young innocent through manipulation that spans gentle flattery to outright bullying and everywhere in between. Today, the term "svengali" refers to a person who uses emotional abuse to control another (usually someone younger, creative and innocent/naïve) through manipulation in much the same way as du Maurier's character.

The popular 1990's television show, *Seinfeld*, used the term "svengali" in an episode where Elaine, played by Julia Louis-Dreyfus, is dating her psychiatrist. He is controlling her and she knows it. But every time she tries to end the relationship, he talks her out of it. Manipulates her. She tries to end it by introducing him to her new boyfriend. But her svengali manages to convince her boyfriend to break up with her! In the world of a sit-com, the premise is hysterical. In real life, svengalis ruin people's lives. And anybody those sad (and likely broken) individuals may be connected to.

Even if you've never heard of du Maurier or his novel before, we've all known our share of svengalis. People who bully us. Railroad us. Control us. Convince us that what we know to be wrong, is absolutely right. And there is something really wrong with us for thinking otherwise. Basically, a svengali holds you emotional hostage. The effect is similar to Stockholm Syndrome, where a captive develops love and loyalty for the person holding them against their will. A svengali can make your life hell. And even if you want to escape, unless you take on the svengali directly, which is obviously not easy, you will continuously be drawn back, entangled in their sticky, manipulative web.

Phobia

December 18, 2018

What Is It?

A phobia is a persistent, excessive, unrealistic fear of an object, person, animal, activity or situation. It is a type of anxiety disorder. A person with a phobia either tries to avoid the thing that triggers the fear, or endures it with great anxiety and distress.

Some phobias are very specific and limited. For example, a person may fear only spiders (arachnophobia) or cats (ailurophobia). In this case, the person lives relatively free of anxiety by avoiding the thing he or she fears. Some phobias cause trouble in a wider variety of places or situations. For example, symptoms of acrophobia (fear of heights) can be triggered by looking out the window of an office building or by driving over a high bridge. The fear of confined spaces (claustrophobia) can be triggered by riding in an elevator or by using a small restroom. People with these phobias may need to alter their lives drastically. In extreme cases, the phobia may dictate the person's employment, job location, driving route, recreational and social activities, or home environment.

Specific fears and phobias

Epidemiology and classification

Published online by Cambridge University Press: 03 January 2018

George Curtis, William J. Magee, William W. Eaton, Hans-Ulrich Wittchen and Ronald C. Kessler

Background
Data on eight specific fears representing DSM–III–R simple phobia were analysed to evaluate: (a) their prevalence and (b) the validity of subtypes of specific phobia defined by DSM–IV.
Method
A modified version of the Composite International Diagnostic Interview was administered to a probability sample of 8098 community respondents. Correlates of responses to questions concerning these fears were analysed.
Results
The most prevalent specific fears were of animals among women, and of heights among men. Slight evidence was found for specific phobia subtypes. Number of fears, independent of type, powerfully predicted impairment, comorbidity, illness course, demographic features, and family psychopathology.
Conclusion
Number of specific fears may mark a general predisposition to psychopathology. More detailed information is needed to resolve the question of specific phobia subtypes.

Rape

I cannot even begin to explain the stunned horror I felt after the doctor raped me. It was if I was injected with a mind numbing drug that left me immobile; unable to speak, unable to think. A few minutes prior to his heinous actions, I lay on the table with my heels in the stirrups and legs spread apart. Any woman can tell you that under ordinary circumstances, this is extremely uncomfortable, on many levels; lying flat being one, heavily exposed and vulnerable, another. This examination table was adjusted exactly to the right height, whereby the doctor, after moving my buttocks down to the edge, ostensibly took his penis from his trouser zipper and inserted it into my vagina, very slowly at first. I could not see what he was doing, lying flat, and I fully expected that this was the 'stretching treatment' he spoke of. At some point, I felt a sharp surge of pain, unaware that it was his penis that was moving back and forth with great purpose. He moaned, and it was over. I was stunned. It must have been a few minutes when I noticed him removing his shirt and putting it in his outer coat pocket. He was sweating profusely. I had a moment of clarity just then: He forced himself upon me!

It was at that very instant I felt my soul, my very essence, was stolen from me. I was left immoveable, paralyzed and in a stupor. Nothing was the same after that incident; my thoughts, my actions or my ability to reason, all of those cognitive characteristics which make us human.

He roped me in with the most flattering compliments. He showed me different medical procedures and explained various treatments he administered to some of his patients. He said I was capable of attaining higher goals, as bookkeeping was beneath me. He promised I could be his assistant and one day take over his office. I would be known, by patients, as Dr. Lillian Schaffer. He was a powerful and successful businessman who, through flattery and promises, lured me in emotionally only to be raped, taking my body and soul.

His phone calls the following day found me going back to his office at his command. Dr. Svengali was in complete control. I couldn't engage in conversation, although he tried and tried to have me respond. I felt so strange, as if my body was just a shell and my mind and soul were someplace else. I went back multiple times at his beck and call and was complicit in sexual relations during some of those occasions. I was malleable, easily led, gullible and irrational. It occurred to me if I could get the doctor to marry, it would legitimize my existence. Yes, we could marry for one day and get a divorce. This was the only way to right the wrong which was thrust upon me. This was the only reason, the only purpose I kept a connection with the doctor. Not only was I drawn back to his lair, because of my weakness, but I did not want to jeopardize the possibility of getting him to agree to my plan.

Post Abortion Response

Was I that naïve to think that the doctor was actually going to bring on my menses? What did I do? More egregiously, what in the world did he do? I don't remember much after the intense fear I experienced waiting on that makeshift operating table. I was in a complete haze afterward and throughout the trip home. My thought process was malfunctioning. I remained in a stupor for the next forty-eight hours. It was not for many months that I was able to cognitively conclude that an abortion was performed on me. I continued to live in a trance.

He would call several times after that and I found myself responding to his requests. He would call and I would go. Subsequent to these visits, I endured two more of his 'operations'.

To the all-male jury, this must have seemed a complicit sexual response, but as for me, I might as well have been in a hypnotic trance responding to commands from Svenghali Glickstein!

I was consumed with the notion that if I could get the doctor to marry me, I might regain my position among my peers, as well as my dignity. This would right the wrong that was laid upon me. I might even be reinstated into society as the virgin I once was. As irrational as this was, it was the driving force for the subsequent visits and sexual encounters. There was no gratification during sex, only the overriding voice in my head that said, "Get him to marry you. This will right the wrong." This will reinstate my mind, my soul. This obsession drove me to the doctor whenever he called and asked to see me. Although the consequences were dire, suffering two additional abortions, it didn't seem to alter my fixed thoughts in obtaining what was mine; the essence of who I was. If I had to suffer those sexual encounters and abortions, that would be the price to pay to get Dr. Glickstein to marry me. After all, he was twenty years my senior and already a grandfather and my father's friend. There was no love for him, no devotion. He took what was mine, and I had to get it back. This was paramount.

What Is Posttraumatic Stress Disorder?

Posttraumatic stress disorder (PTSD) is a psychiatric disorder that may occur in people who have experienced or witnessed a traumatic event such as a natural disaster, a serious accident, a terrorist act, war/combat, or rape or who have been threatened with death, sexual violence or serious injury.

PTSD has been known by many names in the past, such as "shell shock" during the years of World War I and "combat fatigue" after World War II, but PTSD does not just happen to combat veterans. PTSD can occur in all people, of any ethnicity, nationality or culture, and at any age. PTSD affects approximately 3.5 percent of U.S. adults every year, and an estimated one in 11 people will be diagnosed with PTSD in their lifetime. Women are twice as likely as men to have PTSD. Three ethnic groups – U.S. Latinos, African Americans, and American Indians – are disproportionately affected and have higher rates of PTSD than non-Latino whites.

People with PTSD have intense, disturbing thoughts and feelings related to their experience that last long after the traumatic event has ended. They may relive the event through flashbacks or nightmares; they may feel sadness, fear or anger; and they may feel detached or estranged from other people. People with PTSD may avoid situations or people that remind them of the traumatic event, and they may have strong negative reactions to something as ordinary as a loud noise or an accidental touch.

A diagnosis of PTSD requires exposure to an upsetting traumatic event. However, the exposure could be indirect rather than first hand. For example, PTSD could occur in an individual learning about the violent death of a close family or friend. It can also occur as a result of repeated exposure to horrible details of trauma such as police officers exposed to details of child abuse cases.

TRIAL TRANSCRIPT PAGES 93 TO 104

By Mr. Conway:

Emanuel Buchholder, being duly sworn, testified as follows:

Q. Did she tell you at that time that on this visit, or one of these visits, when she had gone to the Doctor's office, that he had ruined her? A. Yes, sir.

Q. Did she tell you that he had ruined her by force? A. She didn't mention anything about force.

Q. Did she tell you that it was done on one of these tables that the Doctor has in his office? A. No, sir.

Q. Did she tell you that she had gone there to be treated? A. Yes, sir.

Q. And had been on this table at the time that she was ruined? A. No, sir.

Q. How many times during this conversation that you had with her did she mention the fact that she had been ruined in this Doctor's office, just roughly? A. Just once.

Q. For two hours you say she was talking? A. Yes, sir.

Q. And that is what she was talking about, wasn't it? A. No, sir.

Q. Wasn't she talking about her relations with the Doctor? A. Yes, sir.

Q. Did she talk for two hours about her relations with the Doctor? A. Yes, sir, and a lot of other things in between.

Q. You mean that she broke off what she was talking about and talked about something else and came back? A. No.

Q. Did she talk steadily along on one subject or did she jump from subject to subject? A. Steadily on one subject.

Q. Then what was the one subject she was talking steadily for two hours? A. That she wanted the Doctor to marry her.

Q. She talked about that for these two hours, right? A. Yes, sir.

Q. No feeling? A. Nothing that I could have noticed.

Q. You were looking at her, weren't you? A. I am saying nothing that I could have noticed.

Q. Nothing that you did notice you mean? A. Yes, sir.

Q. Did she say in substance or in words during this conversation that you had with her when she was relating these things that she wanted him to marry her in order to clean up or clear up this sin which she accused him of having committed?

By Mr. Gallagher: I don't want to keep out the conversation bit I want to raise the objection that this is not binding on the issues here.

The Court: It is not proof of any fact at all except there as such a conversation, that is all, it has nothing to do with the truth of any fact alleged to have been stated in the conversation.

Mr. Gallagher: Yes, sir.

By Mr. Conway: Does your Honor overrule the objection? May I go on?

The Court: Yes, go right on.

Q. Did you ever have any other talk with her, Doctor, did you ever have any other talk with her after that day in front of Shraffts? A. After that day?

Q. Yes. A. I had another conversation with her in front of his office the night that he left me to wait for her.

Q. That was how long after that please, Doctor? A. I don't know.

Q. I mean roughly a month? A. Yes.

Q. About a month? A. About three or four weeks?

Q. Then you didn't see her after that, did you, Doctor? A. Not that I could recall.

Q. You don't recall ever seeing her after that time? A. No, sir.

Q. So that for practically a year and a half after this conversation in front of Shraffts, or about a year and a half after that, you didn't see her at all until after this occurrence on December 10th, isn't that so? A. Well, I can't swear to that.

Q. You don't recall ever seeing her? A. I don't recall.

By Mr. Gallagher:

Q. Do you recall anything said in this conversation about other women this conversation in front of Shraffts, did she make any inquiry about other women? A. Not in front of Shraffts, she came to my office and wanted to ask me about that?

Q. Was that after the Shraffts luncheon or before? A. It might have been before and it might have been after, I really couldn't tell you.

Q. She came to your office? A. Yes, sir.

Q. What did she say there? A. She said the Doctor wasn't in so she thought she would drop up and say hello to me, and she asked me, "Does the Doctor go out with any other women, does he love any other women?" or such nonsense, and I said no, he didn't.

Q. You answered Counsel's question here to the effect that the defendant told you at Shrafft's luncheon or outside of Shraffts that she had gone to Dr. Glickstein for treatment? A. Yes, sir.

Q. And that he had ruined her? A. Yes, sir.

Q. Did she tell you what kind of treatment she went there for the first time she went there? A. She said she had a discharge from the vagina.

Q. And prior to that she hadn't gone there for treatment, was that the statement? A. That seems to be her first visit.

By Mr. Conway:

Q. You said she said she went there with leukorrhea, didn't you? A. Yes, sir.

Q. Do you know what leukorrhea is? A. All I know it is some discharge.

Q. Do you know what leukorrhea is a morbid discharge of a white, yellowish or greenish mucus from the female genital organs? A. Yes, sir.

Q. Do you know it is a discharge or inflammation or conjunction of the membranes lining the genital organs? A. Yes.

Q. Did she tell you at that time that on this visit, or one of these visits, when she had gone to the Doctor's office, that he had ruined her? A. Yes, sir.

Q. Did she tell you that he had ruined her by force? A. She didn't mention anything about force.

Q. Did she tell you that it was done on one of these tables that the Doctor has in his office? A.
No, sir.

Q. Did she tell you that she had gone there to be treated? A. Yes, sir.

Q. And had been on this table at the time that she was ruined? A. No, sir.

Q. How many times during this conversation that you had with her did she mention the fact that she had been ruined in this Doctor's office, just roughly? A. Just once.

Q. For two hours you say she was talking? A. Yes, sir.

Q. And that is what she was talking about, wasn't it? A. No, sir.

Q. Wasn't she talking about her relations with the Doctor? A. Yes, sir.

Q. Did she talk for two hours about her relations with the Doctor? A. Yes, sir, and a lot of other things in between.

Q. You mean that she broke off what she was talking about and talked about something else and came back? A. No.

Q. Did she talk steadily along on one subject or did she jump from subject to subject? A. Steadily on one subject.

Q. Then what was the one subject she was talking steadily for two hours? A. That she wanted the Doctor to marry her.

Q. She talked about that for these two hours, right? A. Yes, sir.

Q. No feeling? A. Nothing that I could have noticed.

Q. You were looking at her, weren't you? A. I am saying nothing that I could have noticed.

Q. Nothing that you did notice you mean? A. Yes, sir.

Q. Did she say in substance or in words during this conversation that you had with her when she was relating these things that she wanted him to marry her in order to clean up or clear up this sin which she accused him of having committed?

OBJECTION! Not binding to the issue...?

Opening Address to Jury by Mr. Conway:

Mr. Foreman and Gentlemen of the Jury: You have heard the case for the prosecution. and it now becomes incumbent upon me to do what Mr. Gallagher did about this time yesterday afternoon. You have been told that the defendant went into the Doctor's office at 535 Bedford avenue and fired this shot which very unfortunately resulted in his death, and that she was in such a condition of mind at that time that she did not know the nature or quality of her act, or did not know that it was wrong. In order to establish that, we have to go back a little bit and tell you the story of what it seems to us is the story of a mental disorder, and in talking about it, Gentlemen, I am going to talk about it frankly and in a way that possibly some of my own witnesses may not like, but I want to give you the situation just as I see it, and as I think the evidence will make you see it. Mrs. Raizen, then a little girl, lived in the same house with Dr. Glickstein over on Henry Street on the East Side of Manhattan. Dr. Glickstein had his office downstairs where he occupied the parlor and basement floor, and she, that is Mrs. Raizen and her father and sister lived up-stairs. Her father and Dr. Glickstein were very friendly. There-after Dr. Glickstein came over to Brooklyn and I believe, he was first on South 5th Street and later on Bedford avenue, and her family moved to Henry Street over here in Brooklyn after a while, which is down near her father's place of business, and then late down to Bensonhurst Avenue W so that both families subsequently migrated or came over to Brooklyn.

Back in 1914 or 1915 or 1916 began the occurrences which subsequently, as the evidence will disclose, brought about the condition in this woman's mind which resulted in this awful tragedy. The defense realizes that it was a very very unfortunate occurrence. Back in 1915 or 1916, Mrs. Raizen who was then Miss Schaffer, Miss Lillian Schaffer, had occasion to go to Dr. Glickstein for the grippe and she went to him because he was the family physician, and her father gave him from time to time $100 at a time to treat the entire family, and she went over to him and she will tell you at that time she was taking music lessons, and she had her music roll with her, and the Doctor was out and she sat there, having known his family, and played the piano, and he came in while she was there, and he treated her for this grippe, and he inquired about her other ailments and she eventually told him that she had this vaginal trouble as to which you have already heard something, and he then attributed that, that is he asked her about her menstruation, and she told him that it was scant, and there was this discharge which she had always had, and he attributed this grippe condition to that and said that that lay at the bottom of all the trouble. Subsequently because of that, because of the grippe, she came and made other visits to him at his office, and he told her it was necessary for him to make a vaginal examination.

Some of the things in this case, as I go along, won't be pleasant for me to tell, or for you to hear, but I want to give you the situation as it existed and in order to do so it is necessary to talk plainly because there must be no doubt of nothing left to the imagination here, this is a Court of Justice. On one of the occasions when he had her there for this vaginal examination, she was on one of these tables which appear, or a table similar to the one which appears in some of these exhibits which have been introduced by the District Attorney and there is one in each of these two rooms which I shall show you, which have already been introduced in evidence rather, and that is a table where the person who is to be examined vaginally, lies down and then you will see in these pictures pieces of that table which they call Stirrups. They are metal pieces which are, as I see it, shaped very much like the stirrups which are used when riding a horse and when the person is reclining upon that table backwards the feet or heels are placed by the position in these stirrups so that by that means there is a better opportunity to enable the physician to obtain a vaginal examination. And she will tell you that on that occasion, or on one of these occasions when she went there this doctor suddenly, having her in that position, violated her, ruined her. That she went home, that she was in a very bad condition mentally and physically. Right at this time I might as well go back a bit and begin to tell you about her generally.

This defendant evidently always had what these alienists or men who study mental diseases know or call psychopathic personality; it is also known as a constitutional inferiority. That displays itself in many ways such as a lack of volitional control. People are generally misfits, have large ideas, great plans for themselves, they have peculiarities, abnormalities and are never right emotionally.

The defendant from the time she was a small child—these mental peculiarities of which I speak, may be said to be constitutional in that beginning at some time when this psychopathic personality may manifest itself it cannot be changed, a person may be born with a psychopathic personality or it may come about, as these men may tell you, because of some event which fixes their growth mentally or emotionally or evolutionarily. These people generally have strong likes and dislikes; they lack continuity of purpose, they are irritable. They are resentful, they are quarrelsome, they are impulsive. Any one of these things which these witnesses will tell you about as evidenced in this defendant would in and of itself be sufficient to fix upon her this psychopathic personality. But the combination of the things which I shall show running through our life, in our judgement, the evidence will show, made her what the alienists and those who understand these things even better than I do, say means a constitutional inferiority or psychopathic personality. That doesn't give anybody the right to do anything anymore than you or I had a right to do, but the point I am coming to is this, with that as a base that is a fertile field of weakness, of predisposition as it were, for the invasion of real serious mental disorders just the same as some people may have a predisposition to tuberculosis or something else similar in character because of heredity, training, or method of life, or something else, constitutionally they have that predisposition. The only reason I am talking about this psychopathic personality is not because that deranges people so as to leave them with a defective reason, so that they do not know the nature and quality of their acts, but given that as a base up on that, or with that and with other facts in this case, it is a fertile field for the invasion of real mental disorders, one of which this woman was suffering from and to that I shall come in some little time. These psychopathics are easily swayed by others, they display poor judgement, they have defective power of reasoning.

We say that this woman with this base, this makeup, in this situation which this man, her father's friend, twenty or more years her senior, had with force against her will, ruined her. She went home and stayed up all night. She began from that moment to worry and brood over this thing, and she determined then that night, sitting up all nights, or thereafter within a very short period, she didn't tell her father, she didn't tell her mother, she determined, got the idea into her head that she was ruined, and brought home a towel or napkin with the evidence of her lost virginity, and she kept it for years, kept it right up until some months before this matter happened, or at least it was there when she went down South, as I shall tell you later, which was only about a month before this occurrence, that she kept it locked in a drawer, that all these years she came to the conclusion that the one way she could get that virginity back, or be rehabilitated in the minds of her fellow women, was to get this man to marry her, and from that moment on she determined to go through anything in order to enable her eventually to marry this man and again be able to look her fellow women in the eye because then this virginity which was gone, the sin would be cleaned up, eradicated or what else you please to call it, and she could again walk forward among the other people who hadn't had any similar crime committed upon them.

In order to accomplish that purpose she went back to this Doctor whenever he telephoned her and we shall show that he was telephoning to her two and three times a day during this period over at her place of business, and that when he called up—I told you these people who have those psychopathic personality are easily influenced, easily swayed, she will tell you that although she didn't intend to go to the telephone, nevertheless, at the hour she would find herself there, and she did continue along with him whenever he telephoned, sometimes at frequent intervals, sometimes at intervals not so frequent until 1918 or 1919, and then what happened somebody in the office got her interested in Christian Science, and she will tell you that thereafter she went to the Second Church of Christ Scientists on 67th Street, and she listened to their sermons and discourses, she read their books, the people in her office will tell you that thereafter she carried this Christian Science book, a big book, to her office, that she pestered everybody around the office with her talks about Christian Science, that she told everybody it was a secret she couldn't tell anybody how it was helping her, and by that means she will tell you that when she went to this Christian Science Church she went attending with the older people, sat with the older people wherever they might be in the church, always, as she will tell you, and the evidence will disclose, always turning these things over in her mind, never at peace for a minute. Witnesses will tell you all during this time she sat at her books, posting in the ledger, all of a sudden during this period she got a weeping spell, got up and would go away for a little while and get over it and come back and go on with her work. She didn't dress properly, she cared nothing about dress, her employer threw one of her sweaters, a dirty old sweater that she used to come to work with, in the garbage pail, he said, and she took it out and put it on again, and she wore discarded clothing of her sister, although she was getting a good salary, all the time turning these things over in her mind, going over and over it until she got into this Christian Science back in 1918 or 1919 and then, she says, with its aid she got away from this relation so that instead of being a person who upon a telephone call would appear at this man's office, gradually, or almost right away, she refused to go and managed to stick to it and eventually practically forgot all about it, it didn't mean anything to her, the relationship was gone, and in this Christian Science church one of the doctrines they taught her was that this never happened, it was unreal, the only things real were material things, in other words just the reverse picture, in fact, I believe, they told her that it was one of their doctrines that in order to cure, you have to be reversed, that which is the opposite is the cure.

Among other things they told her this was only a seeming experience with Dr. Glickstein and that if she got it out of her mind it would gradually become a dream which never happened, and that is what in her case happened, by the aid of this going every Wednesday night. During this time she was engaged in music, two nights a week in music school, over at the Christian Science church every Wednesday night, and she was up at one of the places in New York taking lessons on psychology proving just the kind of person I have outlined, big ideas, theories, managing large enterprises, getting all sorts of education she could not adapt herself to. I will have to go back for just a minute. Her husband who sits here evidently listening to me, had been her boyhood sweetheart, they had grown up together since the time they were twelve or thirteen years old, and she was keeping company with him at the time this thing happened which I have related with Dr. Glickstein, and the doctor persuaded her, as she will tell you, that he was not worthy of her, that he was not worth her love, and with this new idea about getting back to the point where she was before this act was committed upon her, she dropped or broke her relations with her present husband. When she got into Christian Science in 1918 or 1919, again her husband, her present husband, who had always intended to marry her, that had always been his dream, renewed relations with her and they were to be married on May 8th, 1921. Mind you, with the aid of the Christian Science she had put these things behind her, what had happened that was gone, that was out of her life.

Now we come to what I have said has been more or less leading up to the events between May 8th and December, when this unfortunate affair occurred. And I want to direct your mind particularly to that, some three or four weeks before her marriage, Dr. Glickstein had been invited to the wedding, he was her father's oldest and best friend, an invitation had been sent to him. In the latter part of March or the early part of April, he telephoned her at her place of business and told her that there was something very important which he desired to communicate to her, that he had received her invitation, or some words in substance to that effect. This thing, through Christian Science, has become practically a dream, she had put it out of her mind, he had no power over her; no effect on her, and she thought that since she was about to be married he was going to say perhaps, I am sorry the whole thing ever happened, the whole relationship had ever occurred, that what was past was past, and she went over there knowing his family, and she had always known them, thinking that possibly the entire family was going to say something with reference to her upcoming marriage or make her some present for her upcoming nuptials, because she knew his wife and daughter. And she got over there that night and instead of this which she had expected, the Doctor endeavored again, as he had before, to break off her relations with her husband and threw her on a couch and endeavored to renew the relations with her, and one of the friends of the Doctor was in the next room and she threatened to scream and she managed to get out of the house and she met a friend of hers in that neighborhood and that friend will tell you her condition which began this story of this mental disorder that night, because after she got out of the house this friend talked to her and Mrs. Raizen said nothing, she got in a number of cars and got off and said that wasn't there she wanted to go, and presented a picture of a person who didn't know what to think or what they were doing, as this woman related. She didn't sleep very much that night, and the next morning, with her marriage a few weeks off, she got it into her head that she wasn't doing the right thing to get married, that she wasn't playing fair with her future husband, that she wasn't a fit person to marry him, this whole thing had come back on her three weeks before her marriage or thereabouts, or four or five, and she didn't know what to do, so she went down to a Christian Science healer, merely going to the church didn't seem to be enough, she was in real sore straits and she went down to a Christian Science healer, Mrs. Loeffler, and told her the situation, what had occurred, that she didn't know what to do, that she was about to be married, that the whole thing had come back on her, and she couldn't think of anything else, couldn't do anything else.

TRIAL TRANSCRIPT PAGES 433 TO 435

By Mr. Conway:

Lillian's Testimony-Meeting with Doctor prior to her marriage

Q. That is, you went down and talked with the Doctor's children and his wife downstairs, did you? A. Yes, I did.

Q. When you say one of the children, do you mean— A. One of the daughters.

Q. One of Dr. Glickstein's? A. Yes.

Q. You say you went in and sat down and talked? A. I talked with them for about three quarters of an hour.

Q. And then what did you do? A. And then the Doctor said he wants to see me, and I went upstairs and, when I went upstairs, he opened the door, and he got all flustered when he saw me.

He says, "Are you in a particular hurry, Lillian?"

I says, "I am not in any particular hurry, Doctor."

"Well, then, just wait here a minute. I will be right up."

He went downstairs, and I don't think he stayed there but just a few minutes, and came up. I don't know if there was anybody else in the waiting room or not. I don't know. I don't remember.

And he took me in, and no sooner did I get inside, than he began to talk. "You are not going to get married. I am not going to let you get married," he said to me. "You know," he says, "that I love you, and you know," he says—I remember his words, Mr. Conway. He says, "You know darn well," he says, "that I love you. You have got to go with me tonight to South America." "Oh," he says, "if I only had that $15,000," he says, "that I lost" —I think he said that "my brother Meyer lost for me in real estate" —something about real Estate—he says, "I would take you right up in my arms right now."

I got a chill all over me. I didn't think that it was that that he wanted to speak to me about. I didn't think it was that.

Q. Yes? A. And I tried to compose myself. It was very hard. I tried to refer to my Science. I tried to hold myself in the truth. It was hard, and he grabbed hold of me and he was going— not he was going, he did fling me on a couch, and I had all I could do to release myself from him, and I rushed for the door. He said, "Don't go in there, Dr. Friedlander is in there." He grabbed hold of the knob, and I commenced to crack my knuckles. He says to me, —he slapped my hands and he says, "Do you do it yet?" And I says, "I am a little nervous," and he says, "you ought to take a good tonic."

Q. What happened after that? A. And then I tried to go around the other way, around the office, and he grabbed me up and he says, "What are you so hysterical about?" He says, "why were you always such a hysterical kid all the time?"

And I said to him—I says, "Do you want to know," I says, "Doctor, why I was always so hysterical? I will tell you," I says, "You saw," I says, "with your own eyes," I says, "that you were dealing with a virgin, and how you did trick me!"

He says, "You are too smart. You answer too much to the point," and then he took me into the other office, and there, there was an operating couch table.

Q. You and he walked into the other room, did you? A. I rushed into the other room, and he rushed in after me.

Q. What room was that? A. The anteroom, the operating room—I don't know. The operating room, I think.

Q. What did they call the room in which you were, in which you say he threw you on the couch on that night? A. I heard it called the consulting room. I used to call it just a room.

Q. You say you went into what room or rushed into what room? A. The operating room.

Q. Then what happened? A. There he tried to fling me—he didn't try, he did with all his physical force—and he was very strong—put me on the table there, and he almost—he had my dresses up—shall I tell everything, Mr. Conway?

Q. Yes. A. He exposed himself and he stood over me and says, "Don't stop me!" I says to him—I held him off and I says to him—I says, "Do you know," I says, "what will happen if I was the foolish girl I used to be years ago?" And he said to me, "I know what would happen," he says.

"At least," he says, "'you and I would have something between us," he says, "that we can love."

Oh, I got away from him then.

Q. On this occasion when you say he did throw you on the operating table, you managed to escape from him? A. I managed to escape untouched.

Q. What did you do then? A. Then I walked around the street, and I said to myself, "What did I go there for? I thought he was going to apologize to me and that he was going to give me a gift.

What did I go there for?" I said to myself—I said, "He is only a beast, that is what he is. He will never be anything different. Right before my wedding!"

Q. That night you met Mrs. Abrams, who was on the stand, did you, yesterday? A. I don't recollect so much meeting her. I know I did meet her. I don't remember exactly what transpired. I know I met her.

WE MARRIED

In spite of my escalating nervousness. In spite of the doctor trying to talk me out of marrying Charles, we married in May 1920. The doctor summoned me a short time before the wedding. I thought that he wanted to extend his good wishes and apologize for the crimes he had committed against me. So I went to his office. He flew into an obsessed tirade, telling me that if he only had that $15,000 that he lost in a bad real estate deal, he would take me up in his arms and...I had to shake my thoughts lose after hearing those unexpected words and tell him that I only came to hear him apologize for what he had done. Of course, he told me not to get so hysterical, as if this was MY doing and then, in a flash, grabbed my skirts, pulling them up...as I tried to fight him off. He exposed himself and threatened, "Don't try and stop me!" I commissioned every last bit of strength I had, and managed to escape, running out the patient exit door.

I tried and tried to use all of my resources in my Christian Science training, but this was to no avail. All of those mental exercises to put bad thoughts out of my mind and other mind controlling maneuvers were not working. I immediately called Mrs. Leffler to plead with her to attend my wedding to Charles. I just couldn't bear to go it alone. I wanted and needed her support. She consented to be there as Charles and I were wed.

We spent our honeymoon in Atlantic City. Charles could understand my moodiness and nervousness before the wedding, interpreting it as wedding jitters. However, he absolutely couldn't understand why I was like this after the wedding was over. As the days went on, my unrest became manifested in twitches, nail biting and general unrest. Charles confronted me about it and I told him the story; how the doctor had attacked me and ruined me. He was stunned and said that he would rather have been killed than hear such a story! He wanted to return to New York immediately. In the days that followed, he forgave me and said we need to look toward the future, not dwell on the past. As much as I tried, I started to have hallucinations. I began to see the doctor's face in Charlie's. This started a trend of irrational behavior that Charles couldn't accept. He sought the advice of a psychiatrist, Dr. Tannenbaum. Events began to escalate quite quickly.

RIGHT THE WRONG
RIGHT THE WRONG
RIGHT THE WRONG

Perhaps the most pertinent questions in the minds of the nine male jurors were: Why did I continue to go and see the doctor? Why did I continue to have relations with the doctor, and why would I bear the suffering of two more 'operations'? This may have been part of the reason I was convicted. Clearly I wasn't thinking rationally. Why would anyone subject themselves to such abuse? My grandest misconception, (formed from a demented state of mind, which was played upon since a young girl), was in the idea that I could regain my position in society, as an upstanding woman only if the doctor would marry me. My concocted plan was to go to Connecticut, where the doctor would be able to get a quick divorce. He then would marry me and subsequently divorce me, but the doctor told me I was a 'silly girl' to think he would marry me. He said, "You are in love with a man and you should go and marry HIM!" He proclaimed that he was already married and even a grandfather. I wanted my body and my soul restored! This was my mantra, to the point of distraction!

There was one occasion, just before my marriage to Charles, that the doctor summoned me. I thought, from the sound of his voice on the phone, that he wanted to finally apologize to me for his egregious behavior, as a good will gesture before my marriage. Instead, this was yet another one of his manipulations and unsuccessful attempts to ravage me again against my will.

Still, I obsessed upon this idea of marriage restoring me to my original state as a proper woman. I would do ANYTHING to keep that hope alive, even suffer subsequent trysts and abortions. I was plagued with the thought of regaining my soul, my stolen life! Even marriage to Charles, to the one and only man I ever loved, could not erase these thoughts! My mind was free falling into the dark abyss of total irrationality.

Trial Transcript Pages 241 to 249

Charles S. Raizen, 1865 Eighty-Second Street, Borough of Brooklyn, City of New York, a witness called on behalf of the defendant, having been first duly sworn, testified as follows:

Direct Examination by Mr. Conway:

Q. Mr. Raizen, the defendant here is your wife? A. Yes, sir.

Q. How long have you known her, please? A. About sixteen years.

Q. Ever since you and she were about twelve or thirteen years of age? A. Right.

Q. At that time did you live in Manhattan or Brooklyn? A. Manhattan.

Q. Did you and she go out together, or did you begin to call on her before the year 1917? A. Yes, sir.

Q. And about when did this calling upon her by you commence,

Mr. Raizen? A. Practically from the time we went to school together.

Q. And that continued along up until sometime in 1917, did it? A. Yes, sir.

Q. About what time in 1917, please? A. The early summer of 1917.

Q. And in 1917 did that calling upon her by you stop? A. Yes, sir.

Q. And was that due to any difference that you and she had— the breaking off of the relationship? A. Yes, sir.

Q. You knew Dr. Glickstein? A. Not intimately. I just knew of him from the Schaffer family.

Q. From the Schaffer family? A. Yes.

Q. Before that time in 1917, when you say your courtship stopped, was it at your request or at your wife's request? A. We just had some differences and I stopped calling, that was all.

Q. That was in March 1917? A. About that time, yes sir.

Q. Before that time had she ever spoken with reference to Dr. Glickstein or going to the theatre with him or going to the theatre with a party? A. Yes, she at one time told me that the Doctor suggested going out together, and I told her that she should find out what show the Doctor wanted to see, and get tickets for the Doctor, Mr. and Mrs. Schaffer, herself, and myself, and then Lillian wanted to go there.

Q. That sort of just petered out and nothing much was said about that thereafter? A. Yes, sir.

Q. In this time that you have known your wife—for the last fifteen or sixteen years, did you say?

A. Yes, sir.

Q. You have noticed her conduct from time to time, I take it?

A. Yes, sir.

Q. You and she used to go to restaurants and theatres? A. Yes, sir.

Q. Did you always have some trouble or difficulty over what you would eat? A. Yes, sir.

Q. Or what she insisted that you would eat? A. Yes, sir.

Q. Was your wife changeable in mood? Was she sometimes gay and would she change quickly into sadness? A. Yes, sir.

Q. Do you remember an occasion at your home one evening when a piece of music was being played, I believe a violin solo? A. Yes, sir.

Q. I direct your attention to that. Will you tell us just what occurred that night, Mr. Raizen? A. I think we had a little gathering over at my house, and everybody seemed to be quite happy, and there was a record put on the phonograph. I think it was a violin solo. After they had played a couple of minutes, Lillian began to cry and insisted that it be taken off.

Q. About how long ago was that, Mr. Raizen? A. Oh, I would probably say about—you mean from now?

Q. Yes, about what year was it, if you can remember? A. Oh, it might have been in 1916 or 1917.

Q. Before March, 1918, while you were courting her, Mr. Raizen, did she lose in weight? A.

Yes, sir, she was losing a great deal of weight.

Q. And that was in what years, if you remember? A. I think it was during the year 1916. 1916 and early 1917.

Q. And how much weight do you say that she lost in that time, please? A. I don't know, but I know she was losing a great deal of weight.

Q. Well, was it about twenty-five or thirty pounds or as much as that? A. Yes, I think it was as much as that.

Q. Is that about what you think she lost during that period? A. Yes, sir.

Q. Was your courtship renewed, Mr. Raizen, after this break in 1917? A. In July of 1920 I received a birthday card from her.

Q. That was in 1920? A. July of 1920, yes, sir.

Q. What date is your birthday? A. July 23rd.

Q. You answered that birthday card? A. I was on my way up to the mountains then, and I replied from the mountains.

Q. Did you see your wife after that? A. I think I did either early in August or September of that year.

Q. What occurred then? A. I met her one evening and we went for a drive, but I didn't see her again for a couple of weeks after that, and then one time I made up a party with another friend of mine and a young lady that he was keeping company with, and we all went down to the Villepigue for a shore dinner.

Q. Then after did you see your wife? A. Why, yes, I began calling on her again quite frequently.

Q. And the courtship was renewed? A. Yes, sir.

Q. Along in November of 1920, Mr. Raizen, do you recall on occasion when she went to register? A. Yes, sir.

Q. I just direct your attention to that. You recall that, do you? A. Yes, I was at her home just prior to the election of that year, and she went down to register with a Mr. and Mrs. Wallerstein, who lived in the adjoining house.

Q. May I interrupt? I said register in November. I mean at the time she registered for the election which was in November, 1920. A. Well, I think the registration is just prior to the election, isn't it?

Q. Well, it is in October. All right. A. It was just prior—anyways, it was at registration time; I remember that distinctly; and the registration booth was in a garage, a sort of store like, and they had to stand in line waiting for their turn to register, and I could see them through a pane of glass, and I was standing outside at the time and kept looking at Lillian, and I noticed that she had a very peculiar twitch to her mouth. She kept on twitching her mouth all the time. There was something I had never noticed before, so when she came out I called her attention to it, and I thought it was just a habit that she had gotten into, and I told her every time I saw her from day to day, I was going to tap her on the chin so that she should try to break herself of that habit.

Q. At that time you thought this was a habit and that is what you said about it? A. Yes.

Q. Mrs. Raizen's mother died in December of 1920, did she not, Mr. Raizen? A. Yes, sir.

Q. You were present on that occasion? A. Yes, sir.

Q. She practically died in your arms as I understand it? A. Yes.

Q. Did you notice any change in your wife after that, after the death of her mother? A. She became very melancholy.

Q. After the death of her mother, Mr. Raizen, was it that your wedding date was set? A. Yes, sir.

Q. What was the date which was set for your wedding, please? A. May 8th, 1921.

Q. Did you notice anything about your wife just before the marriage or just before May 8th, 1921, Mr. Raizen? That is looking back now, do you recall anything that you noticed with reference to your wife? A. She was always moody and downcast.

Q. I mean just before the wedding. Was she forgetful and nervous? A. Of course she was forgetful and nervous, but I attributed it all to the nervousness of the oncoming wedding, that is all. I didn't think of anything else.

Q. When you talked to her just before her marriage, did she answer you? Did she appear to know what you were talking about? A. No, she seemed to be extremely absentminded. I didn't attribute it to anything in particular. I would talk to her and it would seem hard to get an answer out of her, and she seemed to be downcast and downhearted and moody, but I attributed it to her nervousness due to the oncoming wedding.

Q. Did you notice that during the two weeks before your wedding? A. I wasn't here two weeks before my wedding. I only returned about a week before my wedding.

Q. You noticed it during the last week? A. Yes, sir.

Q. You and she were married on May 8th, were you not? A. Yes, sir.

Q. At the Commodore Hotel? A. Yes.

Q. You stayed in the city for a day or two, did you? A. We stayed in the city until Tuesday morning.

Q. And you were married on Sunday night? A. Sunday night.

Q. Did you go to any play or show? A. We went to see "The First Year" Monday night.

Q. That was the night after the wedding? A. Yes, sir.

Q. Is that a humorous or a sad show? A. I thought it was exceedingly humorous.

Q. You had seen it before? A. Yes.

Q. And that is why you took your wife to see it? A. Yes.

Q. Did she laugh? A. No, it didn't seem to be able to get a laugh out of her at all.

Q. The next day you went to Atlantic City? A. Yes, sir.

Q. That was a Tuesday? A. Yes, sir.

Q. Do you remember whether that was in the morning or the afternoon that you went down? A. In the morning.

Q. On the morning train. While you and she were down at Atlantic City, did you and she on one occasion sit down to write letters home? A. Yes, sir.

Q. That was on Tuesday or Wednesday? A. I think it was on Tuesday afternoon.

Q. The same afternoon that you reached Atlantic City? A. Yes.

Q. And did she write a letter? A. She wrote a letter home, yes, sir.

Q. Did you see the letter? A. Yes, I picked up the letter and I read it, and I was struck with the peculiarity of the letter.

Q. Did you speak to her about it? A. Why, yes, in this letter she was writing home she wrote that she was feeling lonesome and she was worried, and I told her I didn't think that was the kind of letter a bride should be writing home. I was surprised at her, and I told her that she ought not to send a letter like that, and she destroyed it and wrote another letter.

Q. What happened next? Tell me in your own way. A. By this time I began to notice the way she was acting. She was so quiet. I talked to her and didn't seem to be able to get an answer out of her, and she had a worried look on her face all the time, and she seemed downhearted and downcast, and I began asking what was the matter, and she simply kept telling me, "Nothing, nothing, nothing," but I wouldn't take "nothing" for an answer, because I could see that there was something that I didn't know what it was, and I think it was late that afternoon or it might have been the following day, that she finally told me about her affair with Dr. Glickstein.

Q. What did she tell you, Mr. Raizen? A. Why, she just told me that on one occasion when she went to see Dr. Glickstein, that he took advantage of her and that relationship continued on for some time, and he told her that because I was sick I wasn't worthy of her and she ought to give me up, and he prevailed on her to do that, and that is why we did part.

Q. You had proposed marriage to her back in 1917? A. Yes, sir I proposed marriage. I was leaving on a six weeks trip through the Middle West, and just before I was going away I stayed up with her and her mother one evening until almost two o'clock in the morning and we talked about that, and I wanted Lillian to get married then, but she put me off. She wouldn't get married.

Q. You and she stayed in Atlantic City after that? A. We stayed for about six days after that.

Q. Then you returned? A. Came back to Brooklyn, yes, sir.

Q. And you took up housekeeping, Mr. Raizen? A. At the home of her—

Q. And went to live with her family? A. Yes.

Q. That was out at 812 Avenue W? A. 814 Avenue W.

Q. That was in what month? A. That was in May of 1921.

Q. After that did you notice any further change in your wife, or what did you notice with reference to her actions after that?

A. She seemed to be forgetful all the time. No matter what you would ask her to do, she would tell you she would do it, and afterward you would find out that it was not done. I would leave a suit of clothes in the morning and ask her to send it to the tailor, and when I came back in the evening it would be just exactly where I left it, and when I would ask her why, she would simply say that she had forgotten it. You would talk to her and wouldn't get an answer out of her at all. You would have to repeat your question all the time in order to get an answer out of her. As she was going around as though she were in a daze. She would put things down, and the minute after she put them down, go looking for them. She insisted on keeping a house account of her expenditure, and if the account was out a penny or two, she would sit down and go over the book as if she were booking for a million dollars.

Q. During this time did you know that she was taking treatment from Mrs. Leffler, the Christian Science practitioner? A. Yes, sir, I knew she was going to Mrs. Leffler, because down in Atlantic City after she told me about this, she immediately wanted to go to the Christian Science church, and we walked out on the boardwalk and found out where there was Christian Science church, and went up. I got her a Bible and bought her some leaflets that she wanted, and on the following Sunday morning we attended the services at the Christian Science church in Atlantic City.

Q. During this time after your return from Atlantic City, were you and she talking about what she had told you down in Atlantic City? A. I couldn't talk to her about it. She was going to Mrs. Leffler, and at one time she came back and said to me that Mrs. Leffler told her not to talk to me about it, that if we talked about it we would be perpetuating it, and that Mrs. Leffler suggested that I do not talk to her about it, so we stopped talking about it.

Q. You and she went over and over this thing down in Atlantic City, didn't you? A. Yes.

Q. And then when you came back with her to Brooklyn, you had told her that what was past was past and that you would forgive her? A. Yes.

Q. And that you and she would try to forget? Right? A. Yes, sir.

Q. After that did you visit or become a patient of a doctor yourself? A. Why, yes, I worried a good deal about this thing myself, and it began to sort of manifest itself in a worried look that I was carrying on my face all the time, and just about this time a certain old school teacher came down to see me, who was in the insurance business, and he sold me a life insurance policy, and incidentally we got to talking about psycho-analysis, and he interested me in the subject, and I asked him if he knew of an analyst, and he suggested Dr. Tannenbaum, and I wanted to see Dr. Tannenbaum.

Father's House

Setting up house with Charles proved to be challenging, if not impossible. My problems worsening, I began to have paranoiac episodes, becoming delusional at times. I began to see the doctor's face on Charles and on my father. I saw his car pulling up, not that of Charles. My moods became, once again erratic; agitation my closest friend.

Charles began to have frequent appointments with a psycho-analyst, Dr. Tannenbaum. One night, he expressed a desire to have a conversation with me about his visits. I was full of dread, as I was sure his motive was to leave me and end our marriage. After a lengthy stroll around Coney Island, he said that his doctor thought it would be a good idea if I was to schedule a visit as well. Charles desperately wanted me to go and of course, I obliged, being greatly relieved that my marriage was still intact. When I think back on this time, I am sure that Charles told the doctor of my manic behavior, delusions, weight loss and the overall inability to focus on the normal tasks of day to day living. Today it would be diagnosed as a nervous breakdown.

Dr. Tannenbaum recommended a complete change of scenery. A trip to Florida was discussed, and I was to be accompanied by a husband and wife who were friends of the family. At the last moment, they decided to cancel their trip and I was off on my own. As much as the family didn't approve of this scenario, they knew it was imperative that I go, and with Dr. Tannenbaum's approval, I started the journey that was about to be the first leg in a series of remarkable events.

Trial Transcript Pages 561 to 571

Joseph V. Gallagher, for the People of the State of New York:

Benjamin Reass, one of the attorneys for the defendant, Charles Douglas Robbins, first having been duly and publicly sworn, pursuant to the instructions contained in the commission hereto annexed, and examined on the part of the defendant, doth depose and say as follows:

By Mr. Reass:

Q. Please state your name, residence and occupation. A. Charles Douglas Robbins. I am a resident of the City of Chicago, 4733 Calumet Avenue.

Q. What is your business? A. My business is radio.

Q. Connected with what concern? A. Radio supplies.

Q. With whom are you employed? A. Chicago Electrical Supply Company.

Q. Where are they? A. 360 West Madison Street, Chicago, Illinois.

Q. How old are you? A. Eighteen years old.

Q. I think you were at school until recently? A. Yes, sir.

Q. What school? A. The last school?

Q. Yes, sir? A. The Dodge Radio Institute at Valparaiso.

Q. And where did you first meet the defendant, Lillian S. Raizen? A. I met her, I met the defendant, Lillian S. Raizen in the City of Atlanta, on the route from Boston to Savannah, Georgia.

Q. The City of Atlanta is a steamship? A. Yes, sir.

Q. You met her on the boat? A. Yes, sir.

Q. You met her before that time? A. No, sir, never met her before.

Q. Knew any one that had any acquaintance with, or knowledge of her? A. No.

Q. It is correct to say that you had no information or knowledge concerning this defendant until the occasion when you happened to meet her on the Steamship, the City of Atlanta? A. That is when I met her.

Q. When was that? A. The date I don't remember.

Q. Can you approximate it in some way? Tell us about when it was. A. It was a couple of months before Christmas. I wouldn't swear to that being a fact. That is the best that I can remember, it was before Christmas.

Q. Well, will you say it was sometime in the month of November, 1921? A. Yes, sir.

Q. What was the occasion of your first meeting the defendant on the boat? A. Why, they gave me a little card party on the boat.

Q. Who was with you? A. At the time, my mother. That is all, excepting the rest of the people at the card party.

Q. They were all passengers, of course, on the boat? A. Passengers, yes, sir.

Q. Your mother is Mary E. Robbins? A. Yes, sir.

Q. Well, now, tell us in your own way just what transpired at that time, in substance. A. Well, I met her at this card party, and she was the only person that was on the boat that was young at all, that attracted my attention, in that I believed that I would like to associate with and I don't know exactly why, but it was the acquaintance with her, and I got to talking with her on the boat and she told me her whole story. She seemed to be troubled, she seemed to be troubled about some man, I have forgotten his name.

Q. Did your mother meet her at the same time that you met her? A. Yes, sir.

Q. What was the conversation? A. And in the conversation she insisted on bringing this man up, she insisted on talking about this man continually, and I would talk with her there, I was talking with her there from eight o'clock in the evening until about one o'clock in the morning, on the boat, and she talked continuously, and occasionally I tried to change the subject and I would change the subject, and she didn't seem to hear at all. She continued to talk about this man.

Q. Now, tell us, Mr. Robbins, just what she said in substance; I don't want you to repeat all what she said in that time, from eight o'clock until one in the morning. Tell us the substance of what she said. A. The substance was that this man had deceived her, that she couldn't seem to discard this man from her mind, she was continuously thinking about him, and she was under the treatment of a psycho-analysis, and he had advised that she leave New York, where she was up north, and take this trip to Daytona and meet some friends on the way, to enable her to try to forget this man. But it seems the harder she tried to forget this man the less success she had and she said when she would wake up in the morning, she would have illusions of this man, that she would wake up in the morning and that she would see this man and she also said that she felt that the way she would discard this man from her mind was to murder him, she thought if she killed him that she could het off her mind. She said that the psycho—the tutor she was under in psychoanalysis told her not to do it, that it would only probably cause more trouble and that she would have this man on her mind stronger after that. For that reason she left New York and was touring the south. She could not get rid of this man, and she left her husband, and she loved her husband, and it was for his sake she was going to forget this man and go South. She also mentioned that she—she said she would be willing to pay for a job if she could get some work in Daytona to try and discard her attention from thinking about this man. She quoted several times that she had illusions of this man, she would see him, and he seemed to have some control or some power over her, and could keep her from forgetting him. She couldn't get rid of thinking of this man. She told me that the main reason she was against this man was that he had deceived her, and after he had courted her—she also mentioned that he had courted her for I don't know how long when she was in New York and later she had apparently forgotten the man who is now her husband and that the day before the marriage, just at the point when she was going to marry this man, he came to her and pleaded with her to run away from him and leave her present husband. She didn't do that, but from that time on she—that seemed to be the time it started her mind, wondering about this fellow, and from time on she couldn't seem to discard him from her mind at all. Her sister had—she told us her sister said this fellow had been pleading with her to run away with him and not to marry this fellow. She said he sister had told her that this man had told the same thing to her, and the same thing to several others, that he was a scoundrel and the sister told her to just forget the man and not think about him anymore, and she tried her best to forget the man and did forget, —did everything possible, but it seemed to her impossible to forget the man. That was the subject of the conversation.

Q. Just a minute, did she say all of this to you? A. She said all of this to me.

Q. How frequently did she repeat the same thing to you in the course of this long conversation? A. The topic of conversation—you mean repeat the same thing over and over again?

Q. Yes? A. Why, from eight o'clock that night until about one in the morning she said these things and she would repeat them, and she was talking continually about this man, and she repeated those things all through these hours I was talking to her. Several times, I didn't remember exactly how many times, she repeated them several times, said practically the whole time I talked, and the steward of the boat came up several times and she told the steward of the boat her story.

Q. The same story? A. The same story that she told me.

Q. Do you remember the name of the steward? A. I don't remember the name.

Q. Would it refresh your memory if I mentioned the name of Percy? A. Percy was the name of the steward of the boat.

Q. Tell us the circumstances under which she told this story to Percy? Just how did that happen? A. Percy came up and sat down at the same table that I was sitting in the lobby at that time.

Q. With Mrs. Raizen? A. Yes, with Mrs. Raizen, and I have forgotten what Percy said, if we wanted some refreshments, or anything, and as soon as she met this steward, she started to tell him the same thing she told me, that this man had deceived her and she could not get him off her mind, and she didn't know what to do about it and she was trying to get rid of it, but she couldn't seem to stop thinking about him, and she had a feeling, she didn't know why, but she had a feeling back in her breast, that she could kill this man, or if she killed him, she would stop thinking about him, that the way to get rid of this man was to kill him, that was very prominent.

Q. You say prominent? A. I mean dominant.

Q. Did she repeat the same idea? A. She repeated that same idea.

Q. Suppose you try to put into first person, quoting her just the language she used when she expressed that idea, as nearly as you can recall, her words on that subject. A. It is hard to repeat the words exactly, but as near as I remember she said if he was dead, out of this world, I think I could forget him. I have a feeling that I could forget him if he was dead and out of this world altogether, but as long as he remains on this earth, I cannot get him out of my mind, I cannot stop thinking about him. Every now and then or every little noise—before I met this man I used to believe everything everybody told me. I trusted everyone, but now anyone tells me anything, I suspicion it, I disbelieve it. Any one tells me anything, I seem to think they are deceiving me too, since I met this man. If he was only out of this world—sometimes when I wake up in the morning I have a terrible strong temptation to kill this man and get him out of the way. I want to get him off the earth altogether. But I know that is not right, and I would not do anything like that. That is the reason I am going south, to forget this man. Besides the steward, she told everyone she met, that she could get in conversation with, she would bring this story up and tell everyone her trouble.

Q. You mean you talked with her father that time? A. Yes, sir, the next morning.

Q. What do you mean you talked with her after that time? A. Yes, sir, the next morning.

Q. What do you mean she told this same story to others? A. In my presence, in the lobby.

Q. Who would she tell this story to? A. Anyone that came up to the table that she was acquainted with, or I heard her tell this story.

Q. How many people did you hear her tell that story to on that trip? A. Well, confidentially she talked with the steward of the boat and the captain of the boat and several others on the boat. She talked about it to two or three others on the boat, and my mother.

Q. In your presence? A. In my presence, I don't recall the names in the passengers but several passengers. I could say there were ten or twenty, everyone that she came in contact with she told her story to.

Q. You were present on an occasion when she told this story

to a group of men on the boat? A. Yes, sir, in the lobby, there were a group of men and women.

Q. How many were there on that occasion? A. Well, there were altogether on the boat, —there weren't many passengers, there were only fifty passengers she told the story to.

Q. In your presence? A. In my presence, in the lobby. It attracted quite a little bit of attention on the boat. Everyone knew of her trouble. She told this many times there.

> Mr. Gallagher: Let me, for the sake of the record, and for the sake of the witness, inform him that he ought to confine himself to what he heard, and not testify as to every— as to what everybody on the boat knew, and to a confidential conversation that the defendant had with the various people on the boat.

Mr. Reass:

Q. Let me direct your attention to this. Did she repeat this story on that trip to groups of passengers in your presence? A. Yes, sir.

Q. How often did she do that? A. Several times.

Q. How often would you say, can you enumerate the number of times? A. Approximately, I heard her repeat this to different people ten or twelve times every day she was on the boat after we had met her.

Q. How many times would you say? A. That would be about three days after I met her.

Q. How many days were you on the boat? A. That would be about three days after I met her.

Q. How many days were you on the boat? A. About four, I believe, and I met this woman—

Q. What was the size and the appearance of the—what was the size and the numbers of the persons in any one of these groups? A. I guess a group of about a dozen people at a time, and at different times there were different people, of course, in these groups.

Q. What, if anything, did she say on these occasions respecting seeing this man? You said something in your testimony about how she sees him? A. She has illusions.

Q. What did she say on that subject? Recall just what she said on that subject? A. She said when she woke up in the morning she would have a vision of this man, and that this vision would have this feeling of wanting—that he had control over her, it was impossible for her to rid herself of the thought of this man, that he seemed to be with her everywhere she went and that was the only way she could rid herself of this person was to murder him or have him murdered.

Q. Did she say that in the presence of these various persons and groups of persons during the three days you heard her? A. Yes, sir, she said that in the presence of these numbers of persons, to me alone, and she repeated this to the captain. What I meant when I said a little while ago that she repeated this to the steward and the captain confidentially, I was there at the present time; there was three or four of us and she was repeating it to me and she repeated it to the captain and to my mother and to the steward; she told her story in detail for an hour's time or two hours, to people in my presence.

Q. In other words, all of these talks on her part you were present at these, and you heard them? A. Yes, sir.

Q. Was the repetition of this story on all these occasions the same as the one you have told us about having occurred on the evening when you first met her? A. Yes, sir, they were repetitions. Her stories were merely repetitions. She said the same thing in all of her stories and just merely repeated the thing that she had said. She told me her story the first night and repeated the story to everyone she met.

Q. Did you observe her when—did you observe her manner and her acts while she was telling the story? A. She seemed to have a twitching or nervousness. She was irrational. If you noticed her closely she would—there was a little nervous twitching to her voice, she had a peculiar pitch, and anyone could tell that she was overcome by something, and she claimed that it was this man.

Q. Did you notice anything about her hands, what she did with her hands while she was telling this? A. Her hands, she would drum on the table, little nervous movements with her hands and her feet.

Q. Did you notice her eyes? A. Her eyes seemed—she seemed to blink her eyes. She looked rather—I don't remember exactly how her eyes looked, but she appeared nervous. Her general manner was of an internal nervousness, that she couldn't get rid of.

Q. Are you able to describe, Mr. Robbins—I realize it is difficult to do, but can you describe her physical gesticulations, her movements, and the actions, and the sound of her voice, while she was talking. A. Yes, sir, it was with excitement.

Q. What degree of excitement? A. It was very noticeable. But anyone that was attracted by this lady, anyone could easily see that she was excited. I don't know exactly how to explain what I have in mind, but she seemed just excited, that is the best way I can explain it.

Q. You said something about the peculiar pitch in her voice. Will you describe that more fully? A. Yes, her voice was very nervous like, and any—as anyone that had some nervous trouble.

Q. Loud? A. No, not necessarily loud, as I remember it, but it was quick and sharp in a way, rather sharp and quick; that is about the best way I can describe her voice.

Q. I am going to ask you some questions now. Try to answer them directly without comment. Did the words and acts of Lillian S. Raizen, that you have testified about, impress you at the time that they were made as rational or irrational? A. Irrational.

Q. And was her appearance at the time, as you noticed it, rational or irrational? A. Irrational.

Q. Where did you see the defendant the last time? I mean Lillian S. Raizen? A. I saw her at the gate of the New Smyrna depot, New Smyrna, Florida.

Q. Were you on the train with her after the boat ride to Savannah? A. Lillian S. Raizen, my mother and I, came down on the train from Savannah, where the boat arrived, we rode with Mrs. Raizen to New Smyrna.

Q. How long a trip is that, about? A. I don't know, but I think approximately about three or four hundred miles.

Q. How many hours would you say that it took to travel that distance? A. I don't remember exactly, it took up the better part of the day. We started in the morning about eight o'clock, and arrived at New Smyrna in the afternoon.

Q. Altogether for how many days did you have this young lady under your observation? A. About four days, three days on the boat and one day on the train.

Q. Did you ever see her after that? A. I never saw the lady after that.

Cross Examination by Mr. Gallagher:

Q. Now, get down to the boat, Mr. Robbins. Were there many young people on the boat? A. No, sir.

Q. How many would you say besides yourself? A. None except

Mrs. Raizen; I wouldn't say that she was young, but there was none younger.

Q. You classified her as a young person that you were attracted to? A. Yes, sir, she was the only young person on the boat.

Q. And as a result of that attraction you struck up an acquaintance with her? A. I was introduced to the lady.

Q. Who introduced you? A. I don't remember who introduced me, only that someone introduced me at the card party.

Q. Did you seek an introduction? A. No, sir.

Q. Did you—did the steward of the boat introduce you? A. No, sir.

Q. What kind of a game were you playing? A. I think we were playing poker; I am not sure.

Q. How many were indulging in the poker game? A. Oh, a party—well, it had started up—we were about—a party of about six, approximately, and it had dwindled down to a party of about four.

Q. Were you playing for money? A. I don't remember. I don't suppose we were. I know we weren't playing—I know we weren't gambling.

Q. Did you have any chips? A. No, we didn't have any chips. We might have been playing penny-anti, but it wasn't over that.

Q. You had a good memory, haven't you, of the events that occurred on that boat? A. In a general way, but not in detail.

Q. You haven't any difficulty in remembering what you testified to here when Mr. Reass was examining you, did you? A. I had a little difficulty in remembering the details, but the general, principal thing that was most important about the conversation. I didn't have any trouble remembering. That is, the feature of our conversation, the topic.

Q. How long did the poker game last? A. I don't remember, a few hours. Three or four.

Q. Was that in the evening? A. Yes, I think it was.

Q. What time did it start? A. I couldn't tell you exactly what time the game started only it was on the second day I was on the boat. The first time I met Mrs. Raizen.

Q. Where did you board the boat? A. At Boston, Massachusetts.

Q. Did you see her board the boat? A. No.

Q. Where was the boat when you first observed her? A. It was sailing between Boston and Savannah.

Q. Could you make it any more definite than that? A. It was about a day's journey outside of the city, or outside of the harbor of Boston, a little over a day's journey out of the harbor of Boston towards Savannah.

Q. Was that the day you met her, the day you observed her? A. Yes, sir.

Q. The evening of that day you met her at the card party, is that correct? A. I don't remember distinctly whether the card party was in the morning or in the evening. I met her at the card party. That was the first time I had observed her.

Q. You just testified, didn't you, that you thought it was in the evening, and it lasted four or five hours? A. I thought it was in the evening; I don't remember exactly to testifying to that, I am not sure.

Q. You thought it was in the evening, after dinner? A. That would not be, clearly, I thought the card party was in the evening that is the afternoon.

Q. Well now, what is it, afternoon or evening? A. I meant the afternoon when I said it.

Q. Was your mother one of the participants in this card party? A. My mother played at the card party.

Q. All the time until the party broke up? A. Yes, sir.

Q. Who else was in besides your mother and Mrs. Raizen, give us the names of those? A. I don't remember the names of the other people, only that they were passengers on the boat. I don't remember the names.

Q. Who introduced you at the party to Mrs. Raizen? A. I don't remember that.

Q. How do you know—how did she know you? Was it a woman or man that introduced you? A. It was a woman that introduced me.

Q. How did she know your name? A. The woman that introduced me?

Q. Yes. A. I had met the woman, we were introduced.

Q. But you don't know her name? A. I don't remember her name.

Q. Was she an old woman, an elderly woman? A. She was an elderly woman.

Q. She met you, but you didn't know her name? A. I know her name at the time, but I don't recall her name now.

Q. Were there any men at the party besides yourself? A. Yes, sir.

Q. Who were they? A. I don't remember the names of the men. I think I met them at the time.

Q. Did you meet them after? A. You mean later, after that?

Q. Yes. A. I saw them on the boat.

Q. Did you learn the names of any of the men? A. Yes, sir, I knew the names of the men at the time, but I don't recall the names now.

Q. Can't you recall any of them now? A. No.

Q. Were any of these men introduced to Mrs. Raizen, too? A. Yes, sir.

Q. They were all introduced to Mrs. Raizen that were introduced, were they? A. We were all introduced around at the party; everyone met every other one at the party.

Q. But you can't recall any of the names? A. I can't at the present time. I haven't thought of it, that is the details.

Q. Well, you haven't a very poor memory with reference to all the statements you testified here that Mrs. Raizen made during the time that you were with her. You recall those very clearly? A. I recall the statements she made.

Q. Now did you refresh your recollection as to the statements afterwards, by talking them over with anybody before you came here to testify today? A. When Mr. Reass came to the city to get me as a witness, naturally we recalled those memories.

Q. That is the Mr. Reass who examined you today? A. Yes, sir. We naturally recall the memories, what transpired before.

Q. He came down to what city to see you? A. He came down to Palm Beach.

Q. He talked over the case at Palm Beach with you? A. Palm Beach, he came down to get us as witnesses.

Q. Had you read anything about the shooting of the man before Reass came down? A. I read a short notice in the paper.

Q. How long did you read that notice was it that you saw Mr. Reass? A. I do not remember distinctly, I would not know.

Q. Give us your best recollection on that? A. I couldn't say positively, but I think it was one or two months.

Q. After you read of the shooting? A. After I read of the shooting; I could not say positively.

Q. During that one or two months that intervened from the time you read of the shooting, and Mr. Reass' arrival in Palm Beach, had you talked over the case with anybody? A. I had talked about the case with my mother.

Q. Anybody else? A. Not particularly, no. My mother was the only one person that knew anything about this young lady. Well, we told my sister-in-law and my friends about the case.

Q. That was after the shooting? A. That was after the shooting.

Q. Had you talked about the case before the shooting? A. Why, I mentioned the lady to my friends, yes, I did, and my mother told my sister-in-law and my friends that she had met this lady.

Q. Did you say anything else to your friends than just simply that you met a lady, a lady on the boat? A. That we had met a lady on the boat who seemed to have a complex over a certain man she was trying to forget, that she was rather a nice lady.

Q. Did you know the name then? A. How?

Q. Of the lady? A. Mrs. Raizen, yes, I knew her name; I knew the name of the lady I am speaking of.

Q. You had no difficulty in remembering her name when you told your friends about the lady you had met on the boat? A. No, sir.

Q. Do you know where she came from? A. Yes.

Q. Where? A. New York.

Q. Did you get her address? A. No, only—the only address I knew was that she came from New York; I didn't know any particular street or home number that she lived in.

Q. Did you get any address as to where she was going in the South? A. We knew she was going to Daytona.

Q. She told you that? A. She told us she was going to Daytona to see some friends there.

Q. Did she tell you what hotel she was going to? A. If she did I don't recall the name.

Q. Had you arranged to meet her in Daytona later? A. No, not that I remember unless we accidentally happened to ride up to Daytona on a little tour.

Q. How far would that tour be, how many miles would that be from your place about? A. Approximately two hundred miles.

Q. Did you take trips up to Daytona from your place, occasionally? A. My family did before. Yes, my family, not very often, but occasionally we would take trips up to Titusville, on business which is only fifty miles from Daytona. Sometimes we would run up to Daytona.

Q. Did you talk over the possibility with Mrs. Raizen of meeting her when you took these trips? A. We talked over the possibility of her coming to Palm Beach and we invited her to come and see us. And before we left Mrs. Raizen, all the same, before she got off at New Smyrna, and the setting and scenery around New Smyrna, and she would come on down to Daytona to meet her friends, and later she would write and let us know whether she would come down or not.

Q. Did she write? A. I don't know whether my mother got a letter or not.

Q. Do you know that she went down to West Palm Beach then, subsequently, did you learn that? A. I never learned that she went to West Palm Beach. I left West Palm Beach—no, I didn't leave West Palm Beach until after I had read in the paper that she had murdered this man. Shortly after that I left Palm Beach. I didn't know that she went to Palm Beach at all.

Q. What time did you usually get up in the morning when you were on the boat? A. I could not say, approximately seven or eight o'clock in the morning.

Q. What time would you retire at night, as a rule? A. It was irregular; the night I sat up with the ladies, I retired about one or two o'clock.

Q. The night you sat up with the ladies, you mean with Mrs. Raizen? A. With Mrs. Raizen, the night she told me her story.

Q. You sat up alone with her and she told you her story? A. No, there were other people in the lobby.

Q. You were separate with her? A. We had a table in the corner of the lobby.

Q. Alone? A. Possibly five or ten or fifteen feet from anyone else.

Q. And that lasted until one or two o'clock you say, in the morning? A. Yes, sir.

Q. Was it as late as two o'clock? A. It was late as one; I could not say definitely. It was either one or two o'clock. I don't think it was past two. It seemed it was one o'clock or about 1:30.

Q. Now, did you start this conversation with her after the card party broke up? A. Yes, sir.

Q. After they had withdrawn, after the others had withdrawn from the card party, you and Mrs. Raizen remained there and talked it out? A. Mrs. Raizen, my mother and I, remained and started the conversation.

Q. And then your mother withdrew and retired, she withdrew, and you and Mrs. Raizen remained alone? A. Mrs. Raizen and I were alone.

Q. And that was the sequence of events, that is, the card party was the beginning of your conversation with Mrs. Raizen, you were introduced to her, then, that is correct, isn't it? A. Yes, sir.

Q. Then following the card party, and following that you had this conversation which lasted until two o'clock, or, after one? A. I had this conversation, yes, sir, on the particular day, with Mrs. Raizen, but very often people would come down during this conversation—you see I was alone with her—very often people would come up to the table and she would tell them her conversation, tell them the story and they would leave, and we would be alone until somebody else came.

Q. It was following the card party that the conversation ensued? A. I don't recall paying any attention to the lady until I met her at the card party, so naturally it followed.

Q. So after you left the card party, you hadn't left her until you retired that night at one o'clock in the morning, is that right? A. I left her a few minutes after the card party, I left her a few minutes and then we had supper.

Q. You had supper in between? A. We had supper.

Q. Did you continue the card party? A. No, we continued the conversation after supper.

Q. And you were with her all evening with the exception of the several intervals that you went away? A. We were with her all evening, excepting the intervals that we went to supper, I was with her continually from eight until I left.

Q. Continually? A. Yes, sir.

Q. Of course you talked about other things besides this man during the period of from eight until one? A. Well, every time I tried to change the topic of the conversation she wouldn't hear what I was saying, and she continued talking.

Q. Didn't it bore you considerably? A. It bored me considerably, and for that reason I changed the topic of conversation—but eventually I was interested in the lady and I was interested in her story when she first told it. After she kept repeating it, it became boresome.

Q. For the five hours she kept repeating and repeating this story to you during the first meeting?

A. Yes, sir.

Q. You got interested in her, did you not? A. I was interested in the trouble, as everyone else was on the boat, not any more than a person, not any more than anyone that was in sympathy with anyone that was in trouble.

Q. Do you know where she had her stateroom on the ship?

A. No, sir, I don't.

Q. Haven't any idea? A. I know it was on the second floor, because I saw her go to the second floor when she retired.

Q. What floor were you on? A. I was on the first floor; that is, I was on a level with the dining room and she was on the top floor.

Q. Did you see any other of the male passengers talk with her alone as you were doing? A. In the lobby?

Q. Yes. A. I saw her talking with three of four. I saw her talking with Percy.

Q. He was not a passenger? A. He was not a passenger.

Q. I asked you whether you saw her talking to male passengers not connected with the staff? A.Not alone.

Q. You were the only male besides—you were the only male passenger that had her alone with you during the three days you were on the boat? A. I was only alone with her that one night when she was telling me her story.

Q. And every one other time someone else was present when you talked with her, is that correct?

A. What I mean was, I was only alone with her for any length of time that one night. I saw her on the boat again in the lobby and spoke to her alone until somebody came up.

Q. How long would these intervals be? A. I couldn't say exactly.

Q. Would they be half an hour? A. I could not say, I don't know. They wouldn't be half an hour, because I would be talking with her, rather she would be telling me about this man again, and someone else would come up, some friend.

Q. And interrupt the conversation? A. No, just listening in. She talked to them.

Q. Then, you stayed there too? A. I would stay there, too, and she would talk to the whole bunch of us.

Q. Did you see any other male passengers do the same thing at any other time, as you described, having Mrs. Raizen alone talking to her, and then somebody else would come up? A. I never noticed any other male passenger doing that.

Q. Can you give me the name of any other male passenger on the trip, that boat, now? A. I never noticed any other male passenger doing that.

Q. Can you give me the name of any other male passenger on that trip, that boat, now? A. No, not that was not connected with the staff.

Q. The staff? A. No, that was not connected with the staff.

Q. Now, you say that these recitals by Mrs. Raizen of her troubles with this man would last an hour or two at a time, is that correct? A. Yes, sir, when she would get anyone to listen to her she would tell the story.

Q. Let me admonish you, now, Mr. Robbins, to answer my questions, if you can, without answering a different question. Your answer there is "Yes," is that correct, is that what you said?

A. Yes, sir.

Q. This conversation, you say, was repeated probably ten or twelve times every day in the three days that you were on the boat, is that correct? A. Yes, sir.

Q. And you were present at the conversation at the time and heard her recite and reiterate and repeat this statement: is that correct? A. Do I have to answer Yes or No?

Q. If you can.

> **Mr. Reass:** Answer any way you want.
>
> **Mr. Gallagher:** If you can.
>
> **Mr. Reass:** Answer any way you want.
>
> **Mr. Gallagher:** Will you please keep quiet? Will you please stop interrupting my cross examination?
>
> **Mr. Reass:** I am not interrupting.
>
> **Mr. Gallagher:** I will ask again if you will please stop interrupting my cross examination?
>
> **Mr. Reass:** That won't go in the County Court, and it won't go anyplace else. You are telling this witness what to answer. The witness said, "Must I answer Yes or No?"
>
> **Mr. Gallagher:** Have you finished?
>
> **Mr. Reass:** Don't pester me. Ask your questions.
>
> **Mr. Gallagher:** I want to remind you, Mr. Reass, whether you want me to talk to you or not. Remember this is all going in the record.

Mr. Reass: I don't care.

Mr. Gallagher: I want you to stop interrupting this cross examination and if you don't stop the cross examination will stop here and I will object.

Mr. Reass: I don't care if it had ceased along while ago.

Mr. Gallagher: I will object to the introduction of this testimony in any court.

Mr. Reass: I don't care what you do.

Mr. Gallagher: Is that your answer?

Mr. Reass: I don't care what you do. It doesn't make a particle of difference to anybody what you do, Mr. Gallagher.

Mr. Gallagher: You talk about stuff and decency, but you don't evidently understand what the meaning of those words are.

Q. Now, Mr. Robbins, will you now say that you heard these conversations repeated ten or twelve times every day for three days that you were on the boat? A. Approximately, yes.

Q. And you were present and heard the conversation each of the times? A. Each of the times that they were repeated; remember, I saw ten or twelve times I heard. They might have been repeated more than that when I wasn't present. That is when I heard it.

Q. And then you took a train ride and finished it with Mrs. Raizen and your mother, after you got off of the boat, which ride was three or four hundred miles long, did you? A. I was on the train with Mrs. Raizen.

Q. Did you invite Mrs. Raizen to accompany you on the train for that trip? A. My mother did.

Q. Who sat with Mrs. Raizen on the trip in the seat in the car? A. We didn't sit in the same seat all the time. We were in two seats there. Part of the time my mother sat with her and part of the time I sat with her.

Q. During the time you were seated with her how much of these three or four hours, or almost a day, you said, was consumed, would you say? A. You mean by that, how much of the time I sat with Mrs. Raizen on the train?

Q. Yes. A. My mother, Mrs. Raizen and I were sitting in these two booths there, I was sitting with Mrs. Raizen, or my mother was sitting with Mrs. Raizen, from the time we got on the train until the time we left her at New Smyrna.

Q. How were those booths arranged? A. Just like, these train chairs, facing so the backs were open, so that the party sits— and could be occupied by the same party—so that the two seats could be occupied by the same party.

Q. That is, the two seats were facing each other? A. So that a party could be together.

Q. It was an ordinary passenger coach? A. It was an ordinary passenger coach.

Q. The trip occupied about a day, did it? A. Approximately.

Q. And during that time, you were conversing all the time with Mrs. Raizen, you or your mother? A. Mrs. Raizen would continue to tell us the story about this man, continue to repeat her story about this man, several times on the train.

Q. What else was discussed besides that during the whole day on the train? A. Nothing that I remember. The topic of conversation was about this man that deceived Mrs. Raizen. She was thinking about him and no other principal topic of conversation aside from that subject was discussed.

Q. Can you give us any other conversation, whether it was principal conversation or not? A.

Well, we asked the fellow that was selling apples on the train—I had a conversation with him.

He short changed me and I had a conversation with him getting my change back.

Q. Is that all you can recall? A. As I said before, I don't remember little details. I don't remember any little conversation. I mean to say there was no principal topic of conversation the whole day on the train except Mrs. Raizen's case.

Q. And that is the best answer you can make to that? A. Yes, sir.

Q. Did she talk about what she had been working at, or anything about herself? A. In connection with the story about this man, she told us that before she met him she held down a steady position.

Q. Yes; did she say anything else about that? A. No, sir.

Q. What language did she use when she said that the man deceived her; just tell us what she said, what language did she use? A. She used very good English, talked in the English language. She said that this man had deceived her, and that was the principal thought she had in mind about this man, that he had deceived her, and that he had an influence or control over her and that she couldn't get rid of him.

Q. Did you say here today that she told you he had courted her, and then deceived her? A. He had courted her and had deceived her. Do you want me to tell you in what way he deceived her?

Q. Yes: did she say anything about that? Just give me what she said. A. She said that the man deceived her, and he hadn't told her that he was married, and that her sister told her that he was married.

Q. Anything else? A. That was all.

Q. What did you say to her statement about his wanting to run away with her? What was that? A. He came to her the day before she was to marry the man who is now her husband. I said the day. I mean a short period of time. He came to her and she was on the verge of marrying this man, she was preparing for a wedding with this man who is now her husband, and he pleaded with her to run away with him.

Q. Did she say that she knew that he was a married man then? A. No, she didn't say that she knew that he was a married

man then. She didn't know he was a married man until after—
I am not sure about that, whether she knew he was married
when she was on the point of marrying her husband or not. I
don't know whether she found out later that this man was
married or not. But she didn't know at the time he was courting her that he was married.

Q. She told you that? A. She told me she didn't know he was
married at the time he was courting her.

Q. You said also that her sister had told her that he had tried
to run away with her. What was that again? Will you repeat
that again? A. That this man had come and pleaded with her
to run away with him, and in that time had started her mind
wondering about this fellow, and she couldn't get him off her
brain, and that he sister had told her that he told the same
things to several other women, the same things he had told her.

Q. Did Mrs. Raizen tell you when this act occurred, between
herself and the man? A. What act do you refer to?

Q. The act when she said that she was deceived by the man?
A. Mrs. Raizen told me that this man had deceived her, but
she didn't mention any specific date, the only thing, only that
he had deceived her before she married her husband, or the
man who is now her husband.

Q. She didn't give you any time, at all as to when it had occurred? A. Didn't, as I remember; I remember her telling me—
I don't remember of her telling me any date when it occurred.

She might have told me approximately the time, of the time in general when it occurred. I don't remember.

Q. Didn't you ask some questions when you got interested in her case, didn't you ask her some of the details yourself? A. No, she didn't give me time to ask her anything; she kept telling me all of the time.

Q. Did your mother ask her any of the details, while you were present? A. Of course, my mother and I would try to inquire into the case, what was the trouble with her, but she would continually tell us about her troubles, and she did most of the talking.

Q. Did you hear your mother ask her any questions at all? A. I don't recall any distinct questions that my mother asked her.

Q. Did you hear your mother try to stop her from the recitals at any time? A. No, everyone felt sorry for the lady, and no one tried to stop her from talking.

Q. You were very much bored by the constant repetition, were you not? A. I eventually became bored by hearing her repeat the story over and over again.

Q. Did your mother appear bored, too? A. Why, everyone got tired of hearing her repeat the story over and over again.

Q. Notwithstanding all this, your mother and you invite her to come in the train with you, and take this long ride? A. Yes, sir, because we liked Mrs. Raizen, she was a very nice character and we didn't dislike her for repeating her story because it was only natural that the story was bothering her so she would have to repeat it over.

Q. Then, you invited her to call at your home? A. To call at our home in order to help her to try to forget this man.

Q. She was an attractive person, wasn't she, in your judgement? A. In my judgement she would not be extremely beautiful of the kind of a girl—she was—she was quite a bit older than I was, but she struck me—she struck me as she struck my mother and myself, as being a very nice refined type of lady.

Q. She played the piano, didn't she? A. I don't remember whether she played the piano or not.

Q. She sang pretty well, didn't she? A. I don't remember her singing or playing the piano.

Q. Didn't you hear her singing on the boat in some songs? A. I don't remember of hearing her singing on the boat or playing the piano on the boat.

Q. Now, Mr. Robbins, you want to answer truthfully, don't you? A. Yes, sir.

Q. That is your best answer, you don't remember whether she sang and played on the boat? A. I don't remember of hearing her sing on the boat.

Q. You were with her frequently during the three days, were you not? A. Yes, sir.

Q. And you heard her recital? A. Yes, sir.

Q. You heard her recite this story at least ten or twelve times each of these days? A. I heard Mrs. Raizen repeat her story ten or twelve times each of those days.

Q. The best answer that you can give to my question is as to whether you heard her play or sing on the boat is that you don't remember? A. You see, it has been several months since this trip on the boat, and I remember distinctly the things—I remember distinctly of hearing her repeat her story of her troubles, but on the amusements that went on on the boat besides this little card game that I was in with her, when I first met her, I don't remember. I know there was singing and playing of the piano on the boat. I don't know who did it.

Q. Did she play an intelligent game of cards, as far as you were able to observe? A. That was when I first met the lady; I don't remember whether she played an intelligent game or not.

Q. Do you recall whether she won or lost at the game? A. I don't recall whether she won or lost at the game. If we were playing for money it wasn't over penny ante, and no one lost over twenty-five or fifty cents. I don't think anyone lost over a dime. It isn't distinctly in my mind whether we played penny ante when we played poker.

Q. Did you talk to the men, too, on the boat? A. The men passengers?

Q. Yes, the men passengers? A. I met several of the men passengers.

Q. Did you learn to know where they were from, any of them?
A. I remember that one of the men was an ex-service man that had been wounded. That attracted my attention and I met the young friend of this fellow.

Q. What is his name? A. I don't remember his name. As I said before, I don't remember his name.

Q. Where was he from? A. He was from, I couldn't say positively, but I think he was from one of the New England states.

Q. You don't know what city? A. I don't know what city.

Q. Now, Mr. Robbins, you testified here that you felt sorry for Mrs. Raizen, and also that you thought it was natural that she would want to talk about her troubles, is that correct? A. I testified I felt sorry for the lady and that it was only natural if she was troubled by this man's visions and allusions, it was only natural she would talk about it. If anyone has any troubles, they like to tell people their troubles, but I don't think she acted natural in her mind.

Q. You think—you thought if she would come down to place and would visit you it would help to get rid of this trouble that she had. That was the reason that you and your mother wanted her to call on you? A. My mother did the inviting, and we thought that if she would pay us a visit, we could start up a little society around the house and get her enough—I mean, start up a little society around the city, and get up enough life to help her forget her troubles.

Q. You didn't think she was insane, did you? A. I thought, as I heard the steward on the boat explain—he and I were talking about the lady and he said that he thought she was "nuts," and I said either "nuts" or something. That is the way I thought.

Q. Where did you hear the word "irrational" used in connection with her? A. I don't remember where I first heard the word "irrational." I have heard it several times in my life. In connection with her, I think I couldn't say positively the first time I heard the word "irrational" used. I think it was in the paper. I heard people speaking about her I don't know whether I heard anyone speak of her—I don't remember when I first heard the word "irrational" in connection with her.

Q. When Mr. Reass spoke to you about her, and about the case, did he use the word "irrational," do you remember? A. I couldn't say positively, but I think—I couldn't say positively.

Q. When she would recite this story she would do so sitting alongside of you, would she? A. Why, she would sit by me for the time and she would repeat this story, but not every time. Sometimes she was sitting across the table and I was sitting at the other end of the table and my mother would be there.

Q. In the train she sat in the seat and she talked about this man, did she? A. She spoke about this man in the train.

Q. So, she remained sitting and would go over the story again and again, is that it? A. She repeated the story several times to me.

Q. Would she do it while she was sitting in the seat? A. Yes, sir, she got up while she was talking about the case, and she would do it while she was standing up.

Q. She also told the story while she was seated? A. She told the story over and over again while she was seated.

Q. Did she show any symptoms or signs of delusions in her motions while she was telling the story? A. I noticed while she was telling the story and while she was telling, while she was retelling this story, that she had a nervous twitching. Her fingers were drumming on the table in the lobby of the boat. She made little nervous movements as though she was nervous.

Q. Was this just nervousness? A. She appeared to me to be nervous.

Q. Did you see her read, at any time during the trip? A. I don't recall seeing her at any time.

Q. Did she have any books with her, did you notice? A. I don't recall seeing her have any books with her.

Q. Did she impress you as being a pretty well-read person? A. She impressed me as being a person who had an education.

Q. She talked well, grammatically? A. Grammatically, she talked well, but it was mostly when she was talking about this person.

Q. She talked fluently, too, didn't she? A. Yes, she talked fluently. At times she talked fluently.

Q. Did she talk rapidly? A. At times she talked rapidly.

Q. Altogether you thought she was a very attractive person, did you not? A. I thought she was the more refined and attractive type of character, but she was suffering from some trouble, some nervous trouble, and she was greatly overcome by this person that she claimed had deceived her.

Q. She told you that she was troubled with nervousness and the doctor that was treating her advised her to take the trip South? A. She told me that the psycho-analyst had advised her to take the trip South in order to forget this fellow that she had lost consciousness in.

Q. You knew that she was traveling alone, didn't you? A. Yes, sir.

Q. You understood—I understood you to say you never saw her after you parted with her, when you got off the train? A. I have never seen, after parting with her.

Q. Sure about that? A. Absolutely, positive.

Q. Did you have any letters from her, personally? A. Not to me, no, sir.

Q. Did your mother? A. Not that I know of.

Q. Did your mother show any letter that she had received from her? A. I don't recall whether my mother did or not.

Q. Give me your best recollection. Can you answer that any better than you don't recall that? A. I don't recall my mother receiving a letter from Mrs. Raizen. My mother shows me very many letters she receives from her friends.

Q. I asked you that before, and I thought you said maybe your mother had, or in substance that; now give me your best recollection. A. My best recollection is I don't think she received any letter from Mrs. Raizen, although she may possibly have done so.

Q. Where is your mother now? A. She was in Titusville, Florida, the last I heard of her.

Q. How long had you been in Boston, before you took that boat? A. Five months.

Q. Were you working up there? A. I was going to school.

Q. Where? A. The Eastern Radio Studio.

Q. Did any of your friends join you, when you got on the boat at Boston, to take the trip with you? A. Only mother, only my mother.

Q. Was this ex-service man that you got acquainted with, did he get on there, at Boston? A. I think he did. As a matter of fact, I think the route was traced from Boston to Savannah. I know this positively.

Q. You know that for a positive fact? A. I know that for a positive fact.

Q. You didn't stop at New York? A. No, sir, not the boat that we were on.

Q. That is the boat that Mrs. Raizen was on? A. That is the boat that Mrs. Raizen was on.

Q. Can you describe this ex-service man to me? A. This ex-service man had a gash.

Q. Keep your voice up. A. This ex-service man had a gash, a terrible gash in his leg, that had been made by shrapnel and I would approximately say he was six feet tall, rather broad shouldered and had a pleasant looking face.

Q. What is the color of his hair, do you remember? A. I don't remember, but I think it was blonde.

Q. Now, about how old a man was he, would you say? A. I couldn't say exactly; I think he was between twenty and thirty, between twenty-two and thirty.

Q. You don't remember his name, now, after talking about him? A. I don't recall his name, although he was a very good friend of the mine on the boat.

Q. Have you ever met him since that trip? A. Not since that trip, no, only he got off in Titusville with us. He was on the train with me and Mrs. Raizen.

Q. Was he talking to Mrs. Raizen, too? A. They were not sitting in the same booth with us.

Q. Who was with him? A. Another fellow that came down on the same boat.

Q. Did you notice him leaving the train with Mrs. Raizen? A. No, he never left the train with Mrs. Raizen. He was seated in a different part, it was someplace else in the train. I don't know where. I remember talking with this man later, after Mrs. Raizen got off at New Smyrna and told him about Titusville, and persuaded him to stop there at Titusville, not with me, but to stop over there because I thought it was a place he would like.

Q. Did he stay there? A. He stayed there.

Q. For how long? A. I could not say how long he stayed in Titusville; he stayed in Titusville until we left for Palm Beach.

Q. How long did Mrs. Raizen stay in Titusville? A. She didn't stay in Titusville that I know of.

Q. What is the name of that place? A. New Smyrna.

Q. How long did she remain there? A. I don't know.

Q. What was the last you saw of her in New Smyrna? A. I saw her going through the gates of the depot.

Q. Who was with her? A. No one.

Q. Did she have a grip or bag? A. The porter was carrying the grip and the bag. A few paces behind her or ahead of her. I don't know, either porter or cab man. I don't know which.

Mr. Gallagher: That is all.

Redirect Examination by Mr. Reass:

Q. You are Southern born, are you not, Mr. Robbins? A. Yes, sir.

Q. Bred and born in the South? A. Yes, sir.

Q. You have been at school until a month or so ago? A. Yes, I have been at school until a month or so ago.

Q. I presume you were up at Boston at school and your mother came to take you home? A. I went to Boston with my mother.

Q. I understood you to say that you had been in school there for about five months? A. Five months.

Q. Did your mother stay with you in Boston? A. She stayed with me in Boston.

Charles D. Robbins

In a haze of good-byes and a several-hour trip to Boston, I found myself on the deck of the steamship, *The City of Atlanta*, which was sailing to Savannah, Georgia. We sailed in the month of November, 1921. There was a swelling inside of me that was about to burst forth. Charles D. Robbins, one of the younger passengers, was the recipient of this eruption.

My only memories of this entire trip were that of erupting emotions, which accompanied the story of how I was deceived, and my persistent obsessive thoughts about the doctor. I laid this on to anyone who was in close proximity and apparently as testified, time had no beginning or end; I prattled on for hours into the earliest part of the day. I paced, my hands and feet were always drumming, drumming, with the need to repeat and repeat my woe to Steward Percy, the captain, other passengers, anyone within earshot. Glickstein was in my dreams, he appeared on the walls of my room, in the faces of passersby, in the everyday comings and goings. He plagued my thoughts.

It was as if my head was going to explode, along with what was left of my mind. I had thoughts of killing him and I did express this. I was desperate, irrational and also capable of killing myself. I just wanted this uncontrollable fury to stop.

According to Charles D. Robbins, I was irrational. I expressed thoughts about doing away with myself, with the doctor, as the only way to end my agony or gain what I had lost. After all, he took my most precious possession; myself. I was mad; insane.

MARY ROBBINS

Mary was so easy to talk to; a kind mother figure. And as I missed my own mother so, that my heart ached in constant pain, I spilled forth the entire story with such an emotional outpour that some of the facts became skewed or confused. She asked me to play bridge with her. I wasn't adept at the game and my mind refused to allow me the concentration I needed. I was extremely nervous and could not control my hands. It was as if they had a separate life of their own. My fingers were in constant motions and if I was near a desk, they always tapped the surface. I almost felt as if all the angst, disappointment, deception and loss were being channeled through my hands.

We were on our way to St. Augustine and for three days I didn't stop. My story flowed out into the heads of practically every passenger. I could not contain myself, the doctor's power held me, and worst of all I felt disloyal to my dear husband in New York. I prattled on in the most irrational manner. I couldn't put my mind to the card games, either Penny Ante Poker or Bridge. I jumped up and left the table after a brief time and headed back to my room. The doctor's face appeared on the wall of my cabin which made sleep impossible. With no desire to eat, my weight started to drop considerably.

The prosecution was trying to make the case that I was fond of the doctor, implying that I was complicit in having sex with him. Of course, I was fond of him when I first came to know him. My entire family was fond of him, and held him in high esteem. My father considered himself to be his dear friend. Fondness doesn't equate to being in love. Fondness was the foundation of the heinous crime of rape that was committed. The fondness was replaced with deception, vile acts of rape, manipulation, abortion and continued bribery and trickery. My sister tried to warn me that other women also fell victim to his ways. She said he was a scoundrel and I should forget him. How can you forget when you are under a hypnotic spell? How can you forget when your mind has been stolen?

I continued to tell versions of my story to anyone and everyone on that boat. Being away from Brooklyn and my family made matters exponentially worse. My nerves, delusions, aberrations and paranoia controlled my existence.

TRIAL TRANSCRIPT PAGES 201 TO 239

Helen F. Weber, of Flint Lake, Porter County, Indiana, aged twenty-five and over, being first duly and publicly sworn, pursuant to the annexed commission, and examined on the part of the defendant, doth depose and say as follows:

Examination in chief by Mr. Benjamin Reass:

Q. What is your name, place of residence and occupation? A. Helen F. Weber, and I live here at Sheridan Beach, Valparaiso, Indiana.

Q. With your father and mother? A. With my father and mother and my baby.

Q. Would it be impertinent to ask how old you are? A. No; I am twenty-six years old. I will be twenty-seven in December.

Q. When did you first meet the defendant, Lillian S. Raizen? A. I met her at the supper table shortly after we arrived in Daytona, Florida, at the Orange Villa Hotel.

Q. When was that, Mrs. Weber? A. That was on Sunday, November 20th.

Q. Had you ever met Lillian S. Raizen prior to that time? A. Never had met her.

Q. Did you know anybody connected or associated or related to her in any way prior to that time? A. No. I had even remarked to her how odd her name was.

Q. In other words, you had never knew or heard— A. Never heard of her.

Q. (Continuing)—her name prior to that time? A. No, sir.

Q. What first attracted your attention to her? A. Well, when I entered the hotel to go to our room that day I noticed her sitting in her room all alone, and after supper I noticed her again. Her loneliness attracted me.

Q. When did you first talk with her? A. Well, we talked with one another at the dining room table at supper time.

Q. Was there anything unusual in the talk that you had at the supper table? A. No; I don't believe I had much time to talk to her then as I was busy with the baby.

Q. You were attending to your child at the time? A. Yes.

Q. Now, did you see her after supper? A. Yes, I saw her after supper.

Q. Did you then have a long talk with her? A. Yes; long talk, considering that I had just met her.

Q. How long would you say that you talked with her that

night? A. Well, I spoke with her; I invited her to go for a walk and we had a long conversation at that time, and then during the evening talked quite a bit later on.

Q. Tell us what she said to you, in substance, and if you can, please use the first person as if she were talking. You see, in other words— A. Quote her?

Q. Quote her, that is what I mean; you have got the correct word. A. I invited her for a walk. I thought she was lonesome and I asked her to join us. I noticed that she was reading a book and she told me it was a—she said: "It is my Christian Science Bible," and I thought it was odd that she being Jewish read a Christian Science Bible and we got into a discussion about it. And she said she had a lot of trouble, "I have a lot of trouble and I find this keeps my mind occupied, because I can't seem to concentrate it on anything right now," And I says: "I think that Bible would confuse you, because I have had some very unsatisfactory experience with this Christian Science," And I said: "In fact a Christian Science practitioner caused all my trouble." "Trouble!" she said, "you look happy." I says: "Well, everyone has their troubles and there is no use showing them theirs." And I told her that a Christian Science practitioner had influenced my husband in a bad way towards his action toward me, and she immediately said: "Do you really believe that anybody could have a spell over anybody else?" And thereupon she told me that she was under a spell—

Q. What did she say about that? Just start in quoting her, just what did she say, as nearly as you can recall? A. Well, she said, "I am a newly married woman, and I am very unhappy although I should be very happy as I have a most wonderful husband—" "Darling" she called him. "But before I married my husband, a man ruined my life." And I says: "As long as you have your husband and you say he is a darling I don't see how it can matter if a man had ruined your life." And she says, "Yes, it wouldn't matter if I was strong minded enough." And she says: "This man has my mind and predominates me every moment of my life. I see him everywhere I go. Everywhere I turn I see him." She says: "At night time I can't sleep." And she says: "When I have—" I told her: "Try to think of sheep jumping over a fence," and all that sort of thing. She said: "I tried and I tried it," she says, "but whenever I get my mind turned into other channels something cold comes over me and it seems as though my breath is being sucked away from me and I have a desire to kill." And she frightened me when she said that.

Q. What else did she say on that subject? Please go right along. A. Well, she just kept on, and I asked her if she didn't have anybody's confidence. She said, yes, she had confidence and she had gone to a doctor's office, who had recommended her coming down here, and I tried to tell her to think of other things and interest herself in many things, and she said, no it was this subconscious influence always getting the best of her, and she could only think of this man and what he had done to her, as well as her family, and she just had that urge to kill is all. She always used the words "urge to kill."

Q. Give us the words that she used when referring to this man? A. Well, she called him a skunk.

Q. Let us have all the words as nearly as you can recollect. A. She always called him a skunk. I never heard his real name. She called him a skunk. She told me he was a doctor but she never mentioned his name.

Q. Give precisely the words as nearly as you can give them what she said with respect to him? A. Well, she always called him a skunk and she referred to him as the betrayer of herself because she said she went to him as a young girl and he had betrayed her, and she would then become very excited and she says, "If only he was only off this earth I think I would have peace."

Q. Have you substantially told us all that she said to you on the first afternoon and evening after your arrival? A. No, we went over—I invited her to go to Realings with me, some very nice people.

Q. That same evening? A. Yes, sir, that same evening, and that is how I happened to get into conversation with her.

Q. Did she accompany you over there? A. She accompanied us. She went up to her room and got a fur and then accompanied us.

Q. What did she say to you then, if anything? A. Well, we introduced her to the people and we were all talking and I had heard of these people before although they were strangers to me, my folks knew them, and she sat so quietly in the room that I tried to draw her into the conversation, but she excused herself to these people and said she was laboring under a terrible strain and that although she tried to get interested in other things this one influence predominated her mind and she began telling her story.

Q. What did she say? A. She began telling she had a lot of trouble.

Q. She said: "I have a lot of trouble?" A. Yes.

Q. Go ahead: what else did she say? A. And "I have been sent down there to try and forget it." And she said: "I know I can't; it is always with me." And she began telling about a man betraying her.

Q. Just use her words about a man betraying her. A. Yes.

Q. Go right on. What I am trying to get is to get you to use the first person, quoting in the words as nearly as you can remember the words. Go on. A. Then Mrs. Realing showed us around the house. I had never been there; it was a very lovely house and we went upstairs and I remember I gave the baby attention up there and she remarked how wonderful the child was and that she wished she could have a child. I remember that.

Q. What did she say about that? A. Well, she said: "I wish I could have a child but I know I can't." She told me—

Q. Did she tell you why? A. No, sir; she never told me why right there, but she told me she never could have a child. Then all of a sudden she excused herself and she said she couldn't stay with us. I tried to coax her to stay. She said; "No, I have to go over to the Christian Science church; maybe my mind might be diverted there by prayer." And she left us and soon after she rejoined us again.

Q. And how long afterwards? A. Well, the Orange Villa was just a few houses away from where we visited and the Christian Science church was just a short distance from there; I imagine it just took fifteen or twenty minutes. She came back and said the Christian Science church was closed on Sunday night. And I was anxious to get to bed, and there were some people there named Pidcock, my mother had told me she understood they were Christian Scientists; I thought they could talk to her because Christian Scientists have a certain way of soothing people, and I said to them: "Mrs. Raizen is feeling very badly, upset;" I said, "try to give her a little confidence in herself." And I—

Q. Was this in the presence of Mrs. Raizen? A. Yes.

Q. Did you say this in her presence? A. Yes, but they seemed to know that she had had troubles too.

Q. Never mind about that. What was said at that time? Was

anything said by them about it or by Mrs. Raizen that you re-call? A. No; she joined them and I retired for the night.

Q. That was the last you saw of her that night. A. That night; yes, sir.

Q. Besides her words and language did you observe anything in her manner that attracted and impressed you? A. Yes; I had a fear of her.

Q. No; no. You are telling us, Mrs. Weber, what did you see her do. Just try to portray for us what there was in her manner and in her actions that attracted you? A. Well, her loneliness attracted me at first, and then after she began to talk to me she was so emotional; she was very emotional.

Q. You are doing something with your hands? A. Yes.

Q. Just tell us. A. She was always doubling her hands up, dig-ging her nails into her palms; and another thing I noticed she had a very bad habit of biting her nails, well, she rather sucked them than bit them, and I spoke to her about it.

Q. What else did you notice, confining your thought for the moment to the first afternoon and night? A. Yes.

Q. What else did you notice in her manner and her actions besides digging her nails into the palms of her hands? A. Yes.

Q. And sucking her fingers in the manner you have described. What else did you notice in her action? A. Well, she was very emotional, and her eyes would almost pop out of her head when she was telling me these things, and she got very excited and would hold her hand to her chest and breathe heavily, and when she explained to me when this cold wave would come over her she would demonstrate it by sucking in her breath, and her eyes would roll wildly, and in a way I kind of feared her just like I would a crazy person.

Q. Was her manner vehement or quiet? A. No, very vehement; she was very loud.

Q. Did you see her the next day, which would be Monday, November 21st? A. Yes, I saw her again just as we were leaving at breakfast time.

Q. Did she talk to you at that time? A. Yes; I said "Good morning" to her. I said: "How did you rest?" She said: "I didn't sleep at all; I didn't sleep at all."

Q. She said: "I didn't sleep at all." A. Yes, she didn't sleep at all.

Q. Did she say anything about anything else to you at that time? A. No; not right then. I went out in the lobby and soon she joined me there.

Q. What did she say to you when she joined you in the lobby? A. Well, I was writing letters and Mrs. Raizen sat opposite me, and she kept up a continual conversation and I was very anxious to write the letters and she interrupted me all the time and she began to tell me about her trouble again.

Q. What did she say? Let us have what she said. A. She said she hadn't slept the night before and she began telling me there was a gas heater in the room and her mind had been in turmoil all the night she thought the only way she could end it was by turning on the gas but she was afraid that the people would find her unconscious before she was dead and she wanted to do it right.

Q. Mrs. Weber, will you be good enough to repeat your last answer and use the language that Mrs. Raizen used; in other words quoting her as nearly as you can? A. Well, as nearly as I can remember—

Q. She said— A. (Continuing) —she said: "I haven't slept right all night. I tried and I tried, and my mind was in a turmoil and I thought at last I would have to get up and turn on the gas and end it all, but the fear that somebody would discover my unconscious body I gave up that idea to find out a more positive way."

Q. Did she say anything else that you recollect at this moment? A. I will try to think.

Q. Just see if this refreshes your recollection, Mrs. Weber. I am handing you a statement that you made shortly afterwards. Look at that last, the second line from the bottom and read along. (Counsel hands witness a paper.)

Q. (Continuing) Does that refresh your recollection of anything else that she said at that time? A. While she was writing the letters?

Q. No, before she was writing; while you were trying to write, besides what you have already told? A. She tried to commit suicide because her mind had been in turmoil all night long, and then she began telling this same story again, that this man had wronged her, and she had this urge to kill all the time that he always predominated her, he was everywhere in her mind, she couldn't keep him out of her mind. She loved her husband. I often asked her if she loved her husband. I said: "Maybe you don't love her husband: that you love this man." No, she said, it wasn't love; it was just hate.

Q. You asked, did she love her husband. A. I asked her, maybe she was infatuated with this man.

Q. Did you ask her whether she loved her husband? A. Yes.

Q. What did she say to that? A. Yes; she loved him dearly.

Q. While she was talking to you at that time; that is, while you were trying to write the letter—were you at that time trying to write a letter? A. Yes; I was trying to write a letter.

Q. To whom? A. I was writing a letter to my sister, Mrs. Louis Gordon, at Whiting, Indiana.

Q. Did you make any reference in that letter to what was transpiring at that time?

Mr. Gallagher: That is obviously objectionable.

Q. Well. Did you make any reference in that letter to what was transpiring at that time? A. Yes, sir. I was—

Q. Just don't tell us about it. A. Yes, sir; I did.

Q. Was that letter mailed by you on that day? A. Yes, sir; I mailed it with several others.

Q. I mean did you mail that letter to your sister? A. Yes, sir.

Q. Did you personally mail it? A. Yes, sir; I mailed it.

Q. Have you ever seen that letter since the time of your mailing? A. Not until just now; no, sir.

Q. It was just shown to you? A. Yes, sir.

Q. In other words, the letter which you wrote at that time— A. Yes, sir.

Q. (Continuing)—and which you addressed to your sister at Whiting, Indiana— A. Yes, sir.

Q. (Continuing)—and which you mailed on that day has been shown to you immediately before you took the witness stand on this hearing? A. Yes, sir.

Q. And you find in that letter the fact that you had referred to Mrs. Raizen? A. Yes, sir.

Mr. Reass: I will have that letter marked for identification, together with the envelope. I will ask you, Judge, to mark for identification these three sheets, together with the envelope.

Q. Did you thereafter again see the defendant, Lillian S. Raizen? A. Yes, sir.

Q. When was that, Mrs. Weber? A. I saw her on several occasions.

Q. Go back again to the morning when you tried to write letters. Besides what you have already testified did you observe Mrs. Raizen doing anything? A. Yes, sir. Mrs. Raizen sat opposite me. This was a low flat desk and she was able to sit right opposite me, and she had a pen in her hand and was writing, too, apparently writing and scratching back and forth, and she would interrupt me and tell me part of her sad story again and then write on her a little bit, and I would let on I didn't notice.

Q. She left you? A. Yes, she went away.

Q. Now did you get up and see— A. Yes, she left her papers on the table and when I gathered up my mail I picked hers up, thinking that she would want it, that she had apparently forgotten it, because she was so excited. And I noticed it wasn't a letter she had been writing but just scratching and figures and odd sentences and phrases, so I just destroyed them, threw them in the basket, because I thought it might embarrass her to have them.

Q. You say "odd sentences." Did you read any of the sentences? A. Yes; I recall one of them was particularly odd, because she said on it "He travels like a donkey," and she had written that down several times.

Q. Did you notice other nonsensical phrases there? A. At the time I noticed them, yes, sir, I noticed quite a few, but I just noticed they didn't have any sense, they were so odd, and that is why I destroyed them.

Q. You don't remember what the words were, do you, besides the one you have already quoted? A. No, I don't think I could; it has been so long ago I really couldn't remember I didn't pay any attention outside of the fact that I noticed they were not anything in particular, just jottings.

Q. Would you say the words that were there and the phrases that were there were meaningless? A. Yes, they were just meaningless phrases. Yes, they were phrases just meaningless.

Q. Did you again see Mrs. Raizen that day? A. Yes, I saw her, yes, at her meals I saw her.

Q. Did you talk to her again that day? A. Yes, I talked with her. We sat at the same table and she always made remarks about the food. Before the food would come in she said: "Here comes the soup that I have had ever since I am here." She said: "They serve the same soup every time." And it wasn't the same soup that we had had the night before, it was altogether a different soup.

Q. Now, did you have any other long talk with her that same day? That night did you have a talk with her? A. Yes, sir; I had a very long talk with her that night.

Q. How long did you talk with her that night, and that would make it Monday night? A. Yes, sir; that was Monday night.

Q. How long did you talk with her then? A. It might have been all of three hours.

Q. Tell us what the substance of her talk was. Use the first person if you please. A. I went to Mrs. Raizen's room to borrow a book and she didn't have any with her. "I haven't any with me," she said, "because I can't concentrate my mind and there is no use taking any along." Then she began telling— and she began telling me her trouble again and this time she went over the same things and would add a few more things for a variation. And she told me—

Q. What did she say, use her words again, try to quote her if you can? A. I am going to tell everything that you are familiar with.

Q. In substance. Tell us just what she said again, in substance, on that occasion. A. She told me—

Q. She said. A. (Continuing) "When I was a young girl—"

Q. She said: "When I was a young girl?" A. Yes.

Q. Go right along now. A. "When I was a young girl I had a certain—" well, I hate to say the phrase, but she had a certain discharge and trouble and her mother sent her to the doctor for medical care, and she said she went there.

Q. She said. A. She said: "I went there, because this doctor was a friend of the family; I had every confidence in him, and he told me it was just a weakness and he examined me and he had me come back time and again and one day he attacked me." I asked her why she hadn't told her father anything about it. She said, because he was such a good friend of the family and she hated to do so, and it was because she didn't tell it first that she never told later on. She said: "He seemed to have a spell over me and I even had to have him at my wedding," she said, "because he belonged—was a friend of my family." She said: "I had a Christian Science practitioner stand next to me during my wedding so that the spell which he had over me would be broken for just this short time, and I thought when I got married that would be the end of this spell," she says, "but it seems as though it had just gotten hold of me and I can't forget in spite of the fact that my husband has begged me to forget and not also ruin his life as well as mine, to start over." And she said: "I try it and then all of a sudden when I am with people it seems as though the room begins to move and then I have this cold chill come over me and then I have the urge to kill." She says: "I can't think of anything, I just can think of this doctor and his face is before me all the time."

Q. Have you substantially told us all of the things that she has told you about this doctor; is that as much as you can possibly recollect, Mrs. Weber? A. Yes. Well, she would even—while we were talking about three hours she told me no details about this doctor, but just told me that he had a family that he was a grandfather in fact, and that he wouldn't leave her alone. When she thought she had cast off this spell, he would call her up and beg her just to see him once more, and she said this terrible feeling that had culminated in this last attack on her life, this spell made her so nervous and made her other than herself, was caused by his calling her up not long before that and asking her to come with him again, and she said that is what she couldn't forgive and she just had the urge to kill.

Q. What was her manner during the time she was recounting these things to you? A. Oh, she was very excited and her eyes would blaze and she had very fiery eyes and those would roll and her voice raised itself so several times I assured her that the people in the hall would hear her; in fact I opened the door at one time to see if anyone was listening out in the hall.

Q. Was her tone of voice very loud? A. Yes, very loud and very excited; in fact, she spoke as though she was talking to an audience instead of me. She was outside of herself really.

Q. Would you say her voice approached a scream at times? A. Yes.

Q. Now, describe her voice again? A. Well, her voice was very emotional and very high pitched for Mrs. Raizen and she was very much excited. In fact, I know in the course of her conversation she partly undressed herself in my presence and didn't realize it.

Q. What do you mean; what did you see; let us know about that? A. She took off her dress and stood in her underwear in front of me. "Well," I said, "you better go to bed." She said she isn't going to bed, and I asked her why she undressed and she said she hadn't realized it.

Q. What did she say now? A. "I hadn't really realized it," she said. "In my excitement I forgot," she says.

Q. Besides the rolling of the eyes and the tone of her voice what other things did you observe in her manner? A. Well, I actually put her down from the time that I met her—

Q. Don't tell us that; don't tell us that. What did you see her do? Try to tell us; describe for us her manner and her appearance while she was telling you these things. A. She had the appearance of a young woman that I had seen that was insane; she just had the appearance of one that was insane on that night and like someone that was very much excited and I would call them crazy.

Q. Did you observe her hands and her arms? A. Yes.

Q. While she was talking? A. She would always clench her fists and she would gesticulate very wildly.

Q. How long did she do this in the course of this two or three hour talk? A. Well, she was doing it most of time of this talk and all this time she was very much excited.

Q. And was that her manner during all that time? A. Yes, that was her manner.

Q. You say her eyes would— A. Her eyes rolled and she would clench her fists and she would talk very loudly and emotionally and she would beat her breast, tell "Here, there was a feeling right here," she said (indicating,) that would overcome her.

Q. You made a gesture. A. Yes.

Q. What was it? (witness indicates)

Q. You are beating your breast? A. Yes.

Q. Did she do that frequently in the course of that conversation? A. Yes, and she would suck her breath in also when she would tell about this and she says this cold feeling came over her and then she would shake her head as though she didn't realize it.

Q. Now it was on the following day, was it not, that you and your father and mother and baby moved your residence from the Orange Villa Hotel to 237 ½ South Palmetto avenue? A. Yes, sir.

Q. Did you see Mrs. Raizen that day at your new place of residence? A. Yes, sir; she helped me carry some of my clothes over to the house from the hotel.

Q. What did you observe her do that night? A. That night she called on us, we had hardly finished our supper.

Q. Just a minute before you write that down. Just before you left the hotel were you and Mrs. Raizen seated on the front porch of the hotel? A. Yes, sir.

Q. What happened at that time? A. Well, I was reading a book, and I had gone out to rather escape Mrs. Raizen because her actions were really annoying me and I sat on the porch and when I looked around Mrs. Raizen came and sat next to me, and she tried to get me in conversation and I tried to interest myself in the book and she just began telling me this same story again, little incidents in it, and all of a sudden—well, I remember I was sitting there, a Franklin automobile passed by, and Mrs. Raizen saw it and she grabbed me by the arm and she said: "Look!" I says: "What's the matter?" And she says: "That Franklin, that's the Doctor." I looked and

I saw it was a Florida license plate and I told her, "That can't possibly be." And then she realized it, too, that it wasn't his, but she told me that he had a Franklin automobile.

Q. Now, did you see her at the house that evening? A. Yes, sir; she came right after supper, after we just finished our supper.

Q. Did you again have occasion to observe her manner and actions and did you again talk with her? A. Yes; she was telling us about what a wonderful husband she had and then how this snake had ruined her life.

Q. Just suppose you tell us again what she said, using the first person, quoting her, what she said? A. Well, I can just recall how this conversation started. I had a little book that I kept a memorandum of my baby's actions and things and there was a misspelled word in it and she called my attention to that misspelled word and then she drew from her purse a letter, which she claimed her husband—she said: "My husband wrote to me when he was traveling," and she said, "I always corrected his misspelled words, so he wrote me this poem." So she read this poem to us which he had written about misspelled words. Then she showed us his picture.

Q. Her husband's picture? A. Yes, her husband's picture, and she also showed us a picture of herself taken with her husband. "See," she said, "that's before I was unhappy. See, what a beautiful girl I was then, how fat and robust and nice." She said: "See, what a wreck this man has made of me now."

Q. Was the picture of the man a picture of a young man? A. Yes, a young stout man.

Q. How old would you say? A. Well, he might have been about twenty four, twenty five, I don't know.

Q. It wasn't a picture of a man of fifty? A. No, sir; he might have been younger; he was just a young man.

Q. He might have been younger than what? A. Than twenty five.

Q. Tell us what she said, if anything, and what her manner and actions were? A. She began telling us of her husband, and she always referred to him as "My Darling" and she began this conversation about this man ruining her life.

Q. Well, did she substantially tell you the same thing as she had? A. Yes.

Q. On the previous occasions? A. Yes.

Q. Was it the same sort of talk? A. Yes, sir; and we were joined by Miss. Realing then, but it made no difference to her, she always kept referring to this skunk, this snake, that had ruined her life.

Q. Did she repeat in the presence of Mrs. Realing what she had repeated several times to you and what you have testified to? A. Yes: this was Miss Florence Realing, and she said the same things to her.

Q. To her? A. Yes, sir.

Q. Were her manner and actions during the repeating of this story you have told the same as you have heretofore testified to? A. Yes, she was very much excited, and in the course of the conversation we spoke of the Ku Klux Klan down here; they had so much trouble, in that year it was, with the Klu Klux Klan and my mother mentioned that, and Mrs. Raizen became very much interested and she—in fact, she insisted of knowing where she could get in touch with the head of the Klu Klux Klan there.

Q. What I am trying to get at, what was her manner during the time that she was recounting or repeating what you have already testified to or what she had already told you on other occasions. What were her manner and gestures? Describe the, if you please? A. Well, her manners were as usual what I have seen of her.

Q. Describe them again? A. They were always excitable and—

Q. What was the tone of her voice? A. Not natural; they were unnatural; they were loud; they weren't considerate of her.

Q. They were loud? A. Yes. Q. What else, they were loud? A. Well, loud and clear, just like she would make these odd motions and hisses and rolling of her eyes.

Q. Did you notice her hands and arms? A. Yes.

Q. How were they? A. Raised and always gesticulating with them and moving them.

Q. That was in the presence of the members of the house and Miss Realing? A. Well, Miss Florence Realing wasn't always there.

Q. Is it a fact that each time she repeated the same story and substantially the same story that she had told you on the previous occasion and about which you have testified and that her manner and actions were the same at that time? A. Yes, sir.

Q. Did you thereafter again see Mrs. Raizen? A. Yes, I saw her.

Q. How many times did you see her after that? A. I saw her the next morning when I went shopping, and that was Wednesday, and I saw her that night, I believe, again.

Q. That was Wednesday night? A. Wednesday night.

Q. Was that the last you saw her? A. Thanksgiving was the last I saw her; that was Thursday.

Q. Now, on that Wednesday when you saw her did you talk with her? A. Yes, sir.

Q. What was the substance of her talk on those occasions? A. I was going down to the town—

Q. Without going into detail, what was the talk, anything like the previous talks? A. Yes; only more excitable yet.

Q. How often during that Wednesday did she tell you her story? A. She told me she was going to commit suicide that morning.

Q. Tell us about that; tell us about that; tell us what she said about the time? A. She said that she had gone—this was rather early in the morning and her hair wasn't combed yet, and I asked her: "Have you had your breakfast?" And she said, Yes. And I said: "I was surprised that you haven't combed your hair." She said: "I went to bed that way and I haven't taken it down." She hadn't really noticed her hair.

Q. Did she say that? A. Yes: "she hadn't noticed her hair." She says; "I have been to the drug store and they sold me some bichloride mercury tablets," and she was all excited about it, and she said, now she can end it. I naturally tried—coaxed her not to.

Q. What did you say? Tell us what you said. A. I said, "You have everything to look forward to;" I said, "any person with as good a husband as you claim yours to be, and anyway, why don't you forget this man and look forward?" She said: "I can't forget it, but he predominates me and at night it is terrible when I see his face in my room it is on all four walls, he surrounds me and takes my breath away." So I was afraid she was going to kill herself, so I happened to remember, I said; "Didn't you read in the paper people that try to commit suicide with bichloride of mercury they usually survive it and they live through all of their life with a terrible stomach trouble because that eats the lining out of their stomach." I said, "Please don't take the bichloride of mercury tablet if you are bound to commit suicide because you won't kill yourself." So she said, well, she would find some way out; maybe if she can, it wouldn't. She would kill herself. I tried to talk her out of it, but she always said there was nothing to live for: that is, she would have something to live for if this man didn't continually follow her around and have this spell on her.

Q. What did she say on that: give us her words as near as you can. Just tell what she said about this man following her around and having this spell on her. Just give her words if you can. A. "I don't have anything to live for, because my darling loves me, but when I am happy, if I am happy for just a couple of minutes and I get him out of my mind, then suddenly he is before me and my breath cuts off, that cold chill comes over me, and then," she says, "the spell is on me again and I can't forget it."

Q. How often did she repeat the same things to you in the course of your conversation? A. She repeated it time and again; she always kept at it.

Q. How many times was it she repeated this to you? A. In this conversation?

Q. Yes. A. She would repeat it three or four, and sometimes five times, I imagine always ended bu there would be an urge to kill come over her.

Q. Give us her words. A. "I have that urge, that urge to kill." And she would gesticulate and clench her fists and fingers, pound her chest, and she would become very excited, the same as though I wasn't there at all; and she would look into space the same as though I wasn't there. She would say: "If I only could forget that spell."

Q. How often would she repeat to you that she was under a spell, this very incident you have testified to, altogether? A.

From the first time I saw her until the end she must have said it at least twenty or thirty times, because that was all she was talking about was this spell that was over her.

Q. You met her first on Sunday, November— A. 20th.

Q. The 20th, and the last time you saw her was when? A. Thanksgiving afternoon.

Q. When was that? A. Thanksgiving, that was on the following Thursday.

Q. Altogether you saw her then Sunday, Monday, Tuesday, Wednesday and Thursday? A. Yes, sir.

Q. Five days? A. Yes, sir.

Q. And during that time how many conversations did you have with her in the course of which she would tell the story that you have already narrated? A. Well, I really couldn't tell. I had only the first—

Q. Just tell us without giving us the details. Tell us the number. A. Well, I really couldn't tell the number.

Q. Well, about how many, give the minimum number? A. Well, it was all of fifteen or twenty.

Q. Was her story on each of those occasions substantially as you have testified to? A. Yes, sir; it was substantially the same.

Q. Was her manner and gesticulations and the rolling of her eyes and her breathing and the clenching of her fists, did they accompany the telling of this story in the manner that you have already testified? A. Yes, sir; always did.

Q. Have you ever seen her since? A. Never seen her since.

Q. Prior to having met her did you ever hear of her? A. Never seen her since.

Q. Prior to having met her did you ever hear of her? A. No, sir.

Q. Pardon? A. I never heard of her.

Q. Is it a fact you were a total stranger to her? A. Total stranger to her.

Q. And to anyone related to or connected with her? A. Yes, sir.

Q. In the course of these few days did you write to anyone concerning these matters? A. I didn't write to anyone right then because she never told me her address; no, sir.

Q. But did you finally ascertain the address? A. Yes, sir.

Q. What did you do when you ascertained her address? A. I wrote to her father and warned him of her having purchased the mercury and of her intention to kill.

Q. When did you write that letter? A. I wrote that immediately upon seeing the notice of Dr. Glickstein's murder in the paper and that mentioned her father's address.

Q. That was the first time you ascertained the address? A. Yes, sir.

Q. That is how we heard of you, Mrs. Weber, wasn't it? A. Yes, sir.

Q. I am going to ask a few technical questions and you answer them without any comment. Did the acts, conversations and manners and gestures of the defendant, Lillian S. Raizen, which you have testified to, impress you at the time when made as rational or irrational? A. Irrational.

Q. Were the appearance which you observed and the acts which you noticed those of a rational or irrational person? A. Of an irrational person.

Q. How were you impressed by the acts and words of Lillian S. Raizen to which you have testified in respect to their being of a rational or irrational character? A. They were irrational.

Q. You mean that they were of an irrational character? A. Yes, sir.

Mr. Reass: Your witness, Mr. Gallagher.

Cross Examination by Mr. Gallagher:

Q. After you wrote that letter to her father Mr. Reass went down and talked to you, in Florida? A. Yes, sir.

Q. This gentleman who is now examining you? A. Yes, sir.

Q. I understood you to say when you first saw Mrs. Raizen she looked lonely and you invited her out to take a walk with you? A. Yes, sir.

Q. And it was at that time that you told her that Christian Science wasn't the thing for her? A. Yes, sir.

Q. She had previously told you that she was going to the Christian Science—or was reading the Christian Science bible? A. I saw her reading it; yes, sir.

Q. And she told you about that? A. Yes, sir.

Q. Then up to that time she had not told you any of her troubles whatever, had she? A. No, sir.

Q. Then you told her that the Christian Science had gotten you in trouble with your husband? A. Yes, sir.

Q. You told her that? A. Yes.

Q. Then you told her what your trouble was with your husband, did you not? A. No, I didn't go into details. I just told her that a Christian Scientist had influenced my husband.

Q. To leave you? A. No; not to leave me.

Q. Well, you told her that the trouble between you and your husband was caused by somebody having some influence over your husband? A. Yes, sir.

Q. You told her that, didn't you? A. I told her that a Christian Science practitioner had influenced him badly towards me; yes, sir.

Q. And then it was that Mrs. Raizen asked you whether anybody could influence a person that way? A. Yes, sir.

Q. You say you didn't go into details about your relationship without your husband but you told her that there was some trouble between you and your husband? A. Yes, sir.

Q. And you attributed it to the Christian Science practitioner? A. Yes, sir.

Q. Up to that time she hadn't told you anything about this man? A. No, sir.

Q. That had the influence over her. So that when you opened the door by telling her some of your trouble she then reciprocated by telling you her troubles. That was the way it came about, was it not? A. Yes, sir.

Q. And you and Mrs. Raizen as a result of your mutual troubles became companions down in the hotel. That is so? A. Not on account of our mutual troubles; no, sir.

Q. It was taken up by you then upon this walk that you invited Mrs. Raizen to take with you, wasn't it? A. Well, I would have invited anybody that I had seen lonely.

Q. I am not asking what you would have done. I am only asking you about the talk between you. It originated on this walk? A. No, I asked her to walk with us because I saw she was all alone and we were familiar with Florida.

Q. You and Mrs. Raizen went alone for this walk? A. No.

Q. Who was with you? A. My mother and father.

Q. Were they walking right with you and Mrs. Raizen or were you and Mrs. Raizen walking by yourselves? A. The Orange Villa is just a couple of houses away from the house where we went to visit Realings, just around the corner.

Q. This conversation which you and Mrs. Raizen had on the first time of your acquaintance was had between you and Mrs. Raizen you both present— A. Yes.

Q. (Continuing) —alone? A. Yes, sir.

Q. That is, separate from others of the party? A. Yes, sir.

Q. Well, Mrs. Raizen seemed to warm up to you, didn't she, she liked you, she apparently like to talk with you, didn't she?

A. She talked to everybody in the hotel.

Q. She did like to talk with you? A. Yes, she was lonely.

Q. And she liked, out of consideration of sympathy you liked to talk with her, too? A. No, I didn't like to talk with her; she became annoying.

Q. All right. But before she became annoying you used to go to her room and talk with her voluntarily? A. Yes, the first time.

Q. You went to borrow a book of hers? A. Yes, sir.

Q. And you talked with her at least fifteen or twenty times during the five days? A. Yes sir.

Q. You didn't try to suppress her, did you, didn't tell her to shut up and keep quiet? A. Yes, we all did; we wanted her to keep still.

Q. I am asking now what you did, not what somebody else did. Did you yourself tell her to keep still? A. Yes, sir, I did.

Q. You still nevertheless would go and join with her and talk with her? A. No, she joined me; I tried to avoid her.

Q. During the talk she said she was a young girl when this doctor attacked her, as you say? A. Yes, sir.

Q. She hadn't told anybody about it at all? A. I believe she had told the other people in the hotel, previous to that in the hotel.

Q. I mean at times these events were occurring with the doctor, she hadn't told at length any time before, her experience with the doctor, had she? A. Her statements were always contradictory; at that time she said, No.

Q. You asked her why she hadn't told her father? A. Yes, sir.

Q. And she said she didn't like to, and then not having told right away she didn't tell later? A. Yes, sir.

Q. That is what she told you? A. Yes, sir.

Q. But she told you then that their relations, illicit relations, were continuing? A. No, that is the impression I had that they were not, that it just had been at one time, one just previous to this one he had called her up again.

Q. Just previous to which? A. To her coming Florida.

Q. Did she tell you that she had relations illicit relations with him before she had come to Florida? A. Not that he wanted to attack her, only he had called her up.

Q. But nothing was done, nothing was done in the way of consummation of the attack? A. No, sir.

Q. So that so far as you could gather there was only one act of illicit intercourse between her and this man and that occurred when she was a young girl, is that what you got from her? A. Well, Mrs. Raizen tried to impress me with that idea.

Q. Not necessarily how she tried to impress you. What did she tell you on that subject? A. Well, that was about all excepting that she said she believed she wasn't the only one with whom he had relations?

Q. Now, I am not asking you about that. I am asking you whether during these fifteen or twenty conversations Mrs. Raizen ever told you about other events, other occurrences, with the doctor similar to the one that occurred when she went there for treatment for this discharge? A. No, sir.

Q. That is the only one she mentioned? A. That is the only time she mentioned excepting that last time when he called her up.

Q. Well, that wasn't complete, that was only an attempt, I understood you say? A. Yes, that is what she told me.

Q. Did she tell you when this first act occurred? A. When she was a young girl.

Q. Did she say about how long ago or give you any idea of the date? A. No, I don't remember.

Q. Did she tell you that from the time of the occurrence of this act that she was troubled with these thoughts about the doctor during the interval or influenced from the time continually when it occurred until you saw her in Florida, that she had this urge to kill, and that she was influenced by this doctor all of this period? A. No, sir.

Q. She didn't tell you that? A. No, sir.

Q. Did you talk to her about that? A. No, I didn't try to be inquisitive.

Q. And she didn't give you any information on that at all? A. No, she just said that her husband and she had been sweethearts all this time.

Q. Did she tell you anything about her life and her work, anything about her life and her work, anything about where she worked and what business she was in? A. I don't recollect; I don't believe she ever told me about her life excepting that her mother died recently.

Q. Didn't she tell you about her being engaged in some mercantile work, in charge of an office or something? A. Not that I recall; no, sir. She didn't tell me anything.

Q. You had all these conversations and she didn't disclose to you her business and work? A. No; she had told me she took singing lessons because she sang, but that was about all. I didn't really know what she did.

Q. She impressed you as being well read and educated? A. Yes, she was well read and educated.

Q. Did she seem energetic and vigorous? A. Yes, she said she would like to engage in some business down there so she could try to forget this.

Q. Did she tell you about her desire to make money and accumulate wealth? A. Yes, she wanted to work in the Ten Cent Store; she was desirous of securing work, I presume, to get this out of her mind. She said it would bet it out of her mind, because she went to the telephone company and offered her services to work for nothing and also in the Ten Cent store.

Q. Did she tell you she had great respect for people who accumulated great wealth in any kind of endeavor that they happened to be in? A. No, in fact I don't think she thought much of money because she wasn't dressed very well.

Q. Did she tell you this doctor was a successful doctor and she admired him because of that? A. No, she didn't talk highly of him.

Q. Did she tell you she loved him at any time? A. No.

Q. I say, did she tell you she loved him at any time? A. No, in fact I asked her if she did.

Q. She told you, however, that he had a family? A. Yes, sir.

Q. That he was even a grandfather? A. Yes, sir.

Q. During the time that you saw Mrs. Raizen, did you hear her sing? A. Yes, sir.

Q. Did you hear her sing at the hotel? A. Yes, sir; at the hotel.

Q. And did she sing over to your cottage too? A. Yes, sir.

Q. Subsequently? A. Yes, sir.

Q. She sang well, did she? A. She sang very well, sweet voice.

Q. In what language did she sing? A. At the hotel she sang in English, she sang a song "In Old Madrid," and at our house she sang a number of Jewish songs.

Q. Did you understand these Jewish songs? A. No, sir, just one I am familiar with, it was "Kolnidre."

Q. You understood that? A. Yes, sir.

Q. You understand the language? A. No, sir; I don't but I know this song; almost all Jewish people are familiar with it, and I am especially familiar with it because the wife of a Doctor Friedman, whom we know, often sang it at her home.

Q. Do you understand the Jewish language yourself, Yiddish?

A. I speak German so I can understand a little Yiddish.

Q. Did she sing other songs in Jewish, too, besides this one you have named? A. Yes, sir.

Q. Can you recall any other songs that she sang in English at the hotel? A. No, sir; just "In Old Madrid"; she sang fifty verses of that, just repeating, she forgot herself.

Q. She played the piano? A. She played piano, yes; it was in the parlor next to the dining room and she used to play for herself.

Q. She used to play and entertain the guests there, didn't she? A. No, she just played to herself and while she was playing some people came in and listened to it.

Q. She played about fifty verses, you say, and sang? A. Quite a number, she kept repeating this "Old Madrid."

Q. Her thoughts were on the piece? A. Yes.

Q. What kind of voice did she have, alto or soprano? A. I couldn't say; it was just a sad—it wasn't—; I would call it contralto I would think.

Q. How long would you say she was engaged in that one song; how long did it take? A. For quite a length of time.

Q. Half hour or an hour? A. No, sir; No sir, just a short song and then she would stop.

Q. Now, the fifty verses, did she consume a half hour in singing those? A. Yes, just the same thing over again, it was just a repetition of "Old Madrid." That is all I remember of the song it is a very sweet little song. Then she stopped and she began telling me of an unhappy love affair that a singing teacher of hers had.

Q. This was another affair, not hers? A. No.

Q. One of her friends? A. Yes, and then she turned right back to this conversation about the doctor, and then she would start right over again.

Q. Did she tell you about anything else, I mean outside of her own affair, anything besides this one this one that the singing teacher had, this affair? A. No, sir; never.

Q. Did she give you this doctor's name at any time? A. No, sir; never mentioned his name.

Q. You understood that she was traveling alone through the south, didn't you? A. Yes, sir.

Q. Did you see any escorts with her down there? A. Never.

Q. Going around the hotel while you were there? A. Never.

Q. Did you see her with any male escorts during the time she was in Daytona before she left on Thanksgiving Day? A. No, I don't believe she knew anybody; there was only one old man at the hotel when we were stopping there.

Q. When you asked her questions did she answer them coherently? A. Well, in our conversation when I would ask her these questions, why she acted this way and why she didn't forget it, she would talk to me and tell me about psycho-analysis and those ideas and she would go off on to a higher thought than I could understand.

Q. Did she talk intelligently about those subjects as far as you could observe? A. Well, intelligently, and still I wouldn't consider it intelligent because I didn't think it had anything to do with what her occasion (was) for being down here.

Q. Did you finish your answer? A. I think I made a bum sentence out of it.

Q. Well, she told you that she was seeking relief from a Christian Science practitioner, didn't she? A. No, sir. She said she was down here trying to forget this doctor, but she was going back because she just couldn't.

Q. Did she say in the first place that she was reading the Christian Science Bible to get some relief from it? A. Not from the Bible.

Q. No. A. No, sir; from this doctor's presence.

Q. Didn't she tell you something about going to another doctor for treatment before she came down? A. Yes, sir.

Q. Did she tell the doctor's name? A. No, sir; she just told me she had to write him letters and tell him how she was progressing.

Q. That he advised her to go South? A. Yes, sir.

Q. Did she tell you that her husband was a patient of that? A. No, sir; she once read a letter to me which she had written to this doctor and it was the same thing that she told me, that she had this urge to kill.

Q. Which doctor are you referring to, the doctor that was treating her— A. Yes, sir.

Q. (Continuing) —for nervousness? A. Yes, sir.

Q. Did she show you some letters that she got from her husband? A. No, there was one letter which her husband had written to her; it might have been before she was married; that is the only letter I had seen that she got from her husband.

Q. Did she show it to you? A. Yes, sir.

Q. Did she let you read it? A. Yes, sir.

Q. You knew her name, didn't you? A. Yes, sir.

Q. You knew her address? A. Yes, sir.

Q. Didn't you know she lived in Brooklyn? A. She told me she lived in Brooklyn; yes, sir.

Q. Did she tell you what her father's name was and his business? A. No, she never did. I tried to get it out of her but I never asked her directly, and I never understood her to say what business her father was in.

Q. Well, any questions you would put to her you got answers to you, didn't you, as a rule? A. Yes, but I wasn't interested enough in her to inquire, you know.

Q. She didn't conceal anything from you, did she when you would put a question to her that was rather pertinent or personal? A. I don't believe so.

Q. So that instead of being that way she was the opposite, she was disclosing matters which you thought she would not have talked about? A. Yes, sir.

Q. When you had all of these conversation [*sic*] about killing and about suicide— A. Yes, sir.

Q. (Continuing)—you didn't attempt to get any address, even of her father? A. I wanted to but Mrs. Raizen disappeared before I had a chance to see her again; we had spoken to my father, and I know I had spoken and said how crazy I thought she was.

Mr. Gallagher: Please don't.

Mr. Reass: Please let her complete the answer.

Mr. Gallagher: Please don't tell what conversation you had.

Mr. Reass: She is going to complete that answer.

Mr. Gallagher: She is not going to complete it; how are you going to get her to complete it?

Mr. Reass: She is going to complete that answer and it is going to go down here; that is all there is to it.

Mr. Gallagher: Are you going to do that physically?

Mr. Reass: No, I am not going to do that physically.

Mr. Gallagher: You are not big enough, and if you are going to do it physically on this hot day you are not strong enough.

Mr. Reass: Mrs. Weber, you want to complete that answer.

Mr. Gallagher: Mrs. Weber, I want you to answer my question and not us about the conversation you had with your father.

The Witness: What was the question?

Mr. Reass: Mr. Commissioner, I am going to ask you to please see that the witness's answer is complete without interference or interruption.

Mr. Gallagher: I don't know how the Commissioner is going to do it.

Mr. Reass: That is his duty according to the commission.

Mr. Gallagher: I don't know how she is going to do it. I am going to object to your questions and I am going to object to the Court to a whole lot of them.

Mr. Reass: That you have the right to do, but that is no reason why it shouldn't be before the court. My position really is that the answer go down the same as the previous question. I may be wrong about it, but that is the correct way, so we can see whether or not the answer is responsive.

Mr. Gallagher: If you don't get so excited and make threats that you are going to do something, perhaps I can get around to it. Let's see if I can meet your objection.

Q. Let me go back to a question or two, Mrs. Weber, before we stopped. I understood you to say Mrs. Raizen would answer questions that you put to her. A. I don't remember of any that I put to her in particular, so I wouldn't say that. I don't remember having asked her questions, maybe I did, but I don't remember.

Q. Now, let us go back. You saw her on Wednesday in the street, the day before Thanksgiving. Was that the last time you saw her? A. No, sir; she was with us on Thanksgiving.

Q. And it was on Wednesday that she talked about suicide? A. Yes, sir.

Q. About the mercury? A. Yes, sir.

Q. And you saw her again the next day? A. Yes, sir.

Q. Did you have her father's address at that time? A. No, sir.

Q. Did you try to get it from her on that day? A. That was Thanksgiving—

Q. Yes. A. (Continuing)—and we had a very good dinner and everybody was talking about the good food.

Q. Was she a participant at the dinner? A. Yes, she was.

Q. What time did she leave that day, about? A. After dinner. I remember taking the baby and pushing him in his cab down the main street and I was gone about two or three blocks when Mrs. Raizen joined me and followed me, and she wanted to wheel the baby and put him to sleep and he eventually went to sleep, and she suggested walking over to the island to see what it was. I had never been over there and it was a very hot day and I refused to walk and when we came back my brother suggested we take the ferry boat and we went over there.

Q. Did you leave her over at the island? A. No, sir; she rode back.

Q. Back to the house? A. Yes.

Q. Back to your house? A. Yes; she rode in the little ferry with us and all this time going back she read me some letters that she had from an aunt of hers, I believe it was in Atlanta, Georgia, I am not sure of the city, I think it was Atlanta.

Q. She was a resident of Georgia, at least? A. Yes.

Q. And did she see them? A. Yes; she held them and she read them to me.

Q. Did you get the address of the aunt then? A. No.

Q. Now, Mr. Reass claimed you were going to say something about some effort you made to get the address from her there; what did you say? A. No, I didn't say I made an effort to; I spoke to my father.

Q. When did you speak to your father? A. Thursday evening.

Q. After Mrs. Raizen had left? A. Yes, I said I thought we ought to try to find out where someone in New York is so we can write them and warn them against her.

Q. You didn't take any steps then and there? A. Yes, I would have done it the next day, but I didn't have a chance to.

Q. I am not asking you what you would have done because that is in the bounds of conjecture. I am asking you what you did do. Now, you didn't do anything until after you heard of the shooting, did you, about writing to any of her friends? A. I couldn't, because that was the last time I saw Mrs. Raizen.

Q. Your answer is, no? A. Yes, and I couldn't.

Q. And so far as you know your father or yourself or any of your family did not take any steps to communicate with the relatives of Mrs. Raizen until after you had read of the shooting of Dr. Glickstein? A. Yes, we saw the address in one of the papers.

Q. Now, Mrs. Raizen impressed you as being a well read woman, you said. Did you see her reading anything during the time you were down there? A. From her conversation I deducted that she had a good education and I saw her reading the Christian Science Bible and she also had a library card that she had gotten a book on and she told me that she just positively couldn't concentrate her mind on reading it, and she gave me this library card because she gave a dollar for it and she said I might get some use out of it.

Q. Did she tell you where she was going from there when she was leaving? A. I never saw her after Thursday; I didn't know that I wouldn't see her, and we got a telephone to come to Jacksonville—

Q. From her? A. No; from Delscher Brothers, a telephone from Jacksonville to come to Jacksonville for our automobile and we left without seeing her.

Q. When you parted from Mrs. Raizen did she say anything about that she was going away on Thanksgiving night? A. No, sir.

Q. Did she tell you at any time where she was going to go in Florida after she left Daytona? A. She was going to try to secure work in Daytona and when she couldn't do that she said she was going to try Jacksonville because it was more of a metropolitan city.

Mr. Gallagher: That is all.

Daytona – The Orange Villa Hotel

There he is! Again! I couldn't help but stare and stare. I swore I saw the doctor behind the proprietor's desk at the Orange Villa Hotel. Every day he showed up behind that desk! Of course Sigmund Freund and his family were quick to notice this constant behavior of staring, because it was unnatural.

It was November 20, 1921 and the Freund family, from Flint Lake Valparaiso, Indiana, were guests at the hotel. I was immediately drawn to his daughter, who was around my age. She came with her sixteen-month-old baby boy. I wanted to be near that child, hold him, give him candy, but every time I approached him, he would get all fussy and refuse my attentions. That child instinctively knew that something was wrong with me. I blurted my story to Mr. Freund and his daughter, Helen Weber. I couldn't breathe, I sucked my fingers and bit my nails. I cried and cried, and it was to these people that I expressed a desire to kill. I had been driven to the brink.

I wanted to kill myself by turning up the gas heater in my room. Fear of someone finding my unconscious body, still breathing, forced me give up that idea. I walked around half dressed in front of Helen Webber. She said my voice was so high pitched and filled with such emotion that I would beat my breast and hiss. I only remembered later that I was cold, so cold and gripped with fear.

The morning found me at a desk scribbling some incoherent phrases. That Wednesday, I went to the drug store and bought some dichloride of mercury tablets to end it all. Helen talked me out of it, saying I wouldn't die, but would have to live with my stomach lining being eaten away causing a lifetime of agony. Life would be grand with Charles, if only I could get away from Glickstein's spell. But this was not to be. Killing was ever present on my mind; killing myself.

Helen's mother, Rosa, was so sweet to me. I was so despondent and she listened to my tale of woe. I told her that Charlie was the ray of sun shining intermittently in my dark reverie. I missed him so. But my lack of worthiness to be his wife was pervading. I felt that my being 'ruined' prevented me from having children. Every time I was near a child, the ever-present sinking feeling became deeper. I ran to Rosa's room, but couldn't stay. I sat down to play cards, only to jump up after a few minutes. My appearance was surely disheveled, but it was not for lack of clothes. They were in a trunk left at the depot, for the past three weeks. It didn't occur to me to go and get it. I also had $300 in my pocket, given to me by my family, but money didn't matter either.

Singing gave me a sense of being in a far-away place. Songs such as 'Illa, Illa', Bohemian Girl and Russian folk songs (sung in Yiddish) told sad stories, and I related to that. But I saw the doctor's face everywhere. He was standing right near me, *telling me to come back to New York*. I was in a present fugue state; a hypnotic trance, under HIS control. Rosa knew I was irrational, by the way I looked and smelled (like a girl from the slums) and acted. She was afraid of me.

My sights were set on Jacksonville. I had to keep running, in hope of alleviating my mental anguish.

JACKSONVILLE – THE ROYAL PALMS

My stay at the Royal Palms Hotel in Jacksonville was amid the most heightened mental turmoil of my visit to Florida. I found it so difficult to stay in one place for any length of time; my room, the lobby, playing the piano or writing at the desk. It was more than several days after my arrival that I tried to get employment at Cohen's Brothers, a wholesale department store. I have no recollection of what transpired or who I spoke with, but I was in no mental state to go to work. That was most likely unsuccessful due to my disheveled appearance and disjointed speech. Testimony from guests stated that when trying to write, I merely ripped up the letter at every turn. I sang in a loud boisterous voice, banging the piano keys, unlike those that testified on the boat going down to Georgia. I couldn't converse on one subject which invariably turned people away from me. This irrational behavior was reflected in my days at the Royal Palms.

Upon my return to the hotel, I ran into Carolyn Bailey. I heard that, in addition to being a Kindergarten director, she was also trained in psychology. I showed her a letter I had received from my psychologist recommending that I eliminate my fears and thoughts of revenge, as if I could wave a magic wand and all that which plagued me continuously would suddenly disappear. I began to pour my heart out to this woman, as my thoughts of revenge to regain that which was taken from me; my chasteness, my body my soul, swelled inside my brain like a pressure cooker spewing steam, screeching and practically shaking me off my feet. Many people testified as to my peculiar murmurings and putting my hands to my head, over and over and over again. I wanted to be the person I was before and was so very desperate to get her back. To me there was only one way to right the wrong, to gain my position in society, to set things right again and that was to kill the doctor. Yes, I admitted this to Carolyn Bailey. It seemed a fair rational exchange in my view: a life for a life. Furthermore, I would be saving other women from this evil doctor, as he had wronged many before ME! I believed this to be true with the little heart I had left, and this was the only way I could go on as the wife to my one true love, Charles.

I needed to find a way, so I engaged the knowledge of Mr. Richardson. As Fanny Foote described him, he was a tall, slender blonde gentleman. He knew a great deal about fire-arms, so we drove to Daytona, about eighty-five miles away, to purchase a gun. I paid him $20 to accompany me.

Trial Transcript Pages 789 to 791
Trip Back to New York

By Mr. Gallagher:

Robert Swayne Perry (passenger on the *St. Louis*)

Q. Were you at the same table with her? A. Yes, sir.

Q. Did you get into conversation with her at all that time? A. Not that I remember.

Q. Did you notice whether she conversed with some of the other guests there, passengers? A. Not that I remember.

Q. Do you remember whether she ate at that meal or not? A. No, not that I noticed.

Q. Did you notice anything peculiar or unusual about her at the dinner? A. Not at that meal.

Q. Did you see her after the dinner meal? A. Yes, sir, I saw her on deck.

Q. What was she doing, when you saw her there? A. She was

sitting in a chair on the deck.

Q. Did you have any conversation with her? A. I was walking on the deck, and as I passed, I made some remarks about the weather or the trip or something, some casual remark, without stopping. That is the only conversation I had with her.

Q. After that, where did you see her? A. Standing at the rail, on that same deck, later in the evening.

Q. Did you have any conversation with her then? A. No.

Q. Well, get down to the time when you first heard her talk, or do something. A. At luncheon, the next day.

Q. Well, what was that? State what it was. A. I asked her—I mentioned the fact that she had not been to breakfast, or asked her why she had not been to breakfast, and she answered me with an explanation. I can't remember the words.

Q. Well, can you give us the substance? A. The substance was that she was not well, or had insomnia or headache.

Q. Any further conversation with her then? A. If so, I can't remember it, the conversation was general at the table.

Q. Did you observe whether she ate anything? A. I did not.

Q. When did you next see her do anything or say anything? A. At dinner that night.

Q. The same casual talk, was it? A. The same casual talk that one has at a steamer table.

Q. Did anything unusual happen then with reference to her, at that meal? A. She was very much brighter than she was at luncheon time, and I distinctly remember she joined more in the conversation at the dinner.

Q. Was her conversation normal, or was there anything unusual about it? A. Her conversation struck me as being somewhat abnormal.

Q. In what way? Tell us what she said. A. Well, I can't remember any single sentence or word that she said, but her conversation struck me as being that of an abnormal person or a person who was in an abnormal condition.

Q. What made you conclude that? A. Just the impression I got.

Q. You cannot give us any basis for it? A. Well, I questioned myself whether she didn't perhaps take some form of drug. That was the impression I got.

Q. She seemed to be exhilarated, did she? A. No, I shouldn't say that.

Q. You say she was more lively? A. Yes, sir; she was more communicative than luncheon time.

Q. Was she at all jubilant, would you say? A. Oh, no; communicative.

Q. You saw her that night later on the boat, did you? A. Yes, sir.

Q. Where? A. Up in the general hall where the piano is, and she sang that evening for us.

Q. What did she sing? A. She sang old folk songs.

Q. Do you remember any of them? A. Yes, sir.

Q. What were they? A. I can't say which evening she sang any particular song, but all the songs were old folk songs, "Dixie," "Old Black Joe," "Nellie Gray," and songs of that type.

Q. Did she remember the words? A. I don't think she ever made a mistake in the words, and she sang a verse of each song.

Q. Did she play the piano herself? A. No, not that I know of. She didn't sing more than one verse of each song.

Q. Did you have music there, notes? A. There was a lady there who was at the piano and seemed to have the gift of accompanying any song.

Q. How did Mrs. Raizen's singing impress you at the time? A. As very sweet; a very sweet voice and a gentle voice.

Q. Did she sing every night of the three nights you were out? A. After the first night—every night, yes. I made a mistake. All that I have described in regard to that singing was after dinner on the second night. It was not on the first night.

Q. Well, was there any singing the first night? A. No. That whole description of mine, with regard to her singing, was relative to the second and third nights.

Q. Well, did you have any conversation with her, any private conversation? A. I never had a conversation with her, except in a group of people.

TRIAL TRANSCRIPT PAGES 327 TO 328

By Mr. Conway:

Isaac Cohen-A passenger on board the *St. Louis* from Savannah to New York

Q. You say you observed Mrs. Raizen on that trip. Will you tell us what you observed about her condition or actions or conduct at that time, please? A. Well, the thing that made the most impression on me was the second evening. I think we were out, and we were having a little concert in the music room, which almost everybody on the boat took some part in or other, and after that concert several of the gentlemen suggested we adjourn to the smoking room and have a little bite to eat, and Mrs. Raizen was invited to join us there for some sandwiches. The different topics, of course, I can't remember now the exact words; it is simply the impression that was made upon me at the time.

Q. What did you notice? First, I want you to do this, if you will, please: what did you observe, first, with your eyes, about her conduct, if anything? A. Well, she was extremely nervous, fidgety, and very generally worked up.

Q. What did you see that makes you say that, Mr. Cohen, please, if you can tell us? A. Well, in the first place, her eyes were roving all over the boat; hands nervous, and unable, except you might say—well, her hands were so that she couldn't hold quiet for a moment. While she was singing on the boat, in the music-room, she several times had to stop and catch her breath. Generally denoted, to my mind, a nervous condition.

Q. When you say she stopped to catch her breath, can you describe that a little more fully than that, please? A. Well, she would be in the middle of a song, or something of that kind; she would have to stop, or did stop.

Q. She did stop? A. She did stop. I won't say she had to stop.

Q. How long would she be stopped for? A. Oh, for a second or so.

Q. This would be in the middle of a verse? A. In the middle of a verse, or at the end of a line, or in the middle of a line, or something of that kind.

Q. Did you have a talk with her at any time, or did she speak to you at any time on the way up, Mr. Cohen? A. Yes, sir, we had several conversations.

Q. You had never seen her before? A. No.

Q. What did she say to you, Mr. Cohen? A. Well, I will try and detail it as much as I possibly can.

Q. If you will, please. What did she say? A. She asked a question of what I would think, or what anybody would think of a man who was a trusted friend of a family, deliberately misusing or ruining a young girl who was a daughter of one of his bosom friends, and then after that, when this girl was trying to break away from his influence, what would I think of a man who would deliberately and maliciously endeavor to hold her in his power. Further, she told me that when she had made up her mind to be married to a young sweetheart, or rather, a sweetheart of her younger days, this man did deliberately try to prevent that marriage, did everything in his power to do so; that he even threatened to go to her husband and tell her husband, or rather, her intended, of the intercourse that they had had and judging from her words, the Doctor had even performed some sort of an operation upon her that would influence the rest of her life. She told me, too, that in endeavoring to get away from this influence, she had consulted Christian Scientists, with a hope that she would be able to turn her mind away from the physical influence that this man had over her, but it was unsuccessful. She went South, at the solicitation of her family, and endeavored there to forget all about it. She was returning, because she felt that being away was doing her no good and she wanted once more to get under the influence of her own husband's family and her own family, but all the time was fearful of what the Doctor would do when she got back, and the principal thing in the whole conversation with me was her fear of the doctor and the influence over her when she once more returned to New York. The thing that made the most impression upon me was that I was a total stranger to her, had never seen her before; she didn't know me and yes as a total stranger she would really unbosom to me the most sacred things in a woman's life. I might say further that this made such an impression upon me that when I got home that evening—

Mr. Gallagher: I object to anything further.

The Court: Yes, I would not tell that.

Mr. Conway: That is all.

TRIAL TRANSCRIPT PAGES 779 TO 781

By Mr. Gallagher:

Lavern Boardwell-Passenger on board the *St. Louis* from Georgia to New York

Q. When did you first notice the defendant on the boat, coming up? A. At dinner, the first night.

Q. Do you recall the date when you took the boat at Savannah? A. I believe, December 7, 1921.

Q. Were you at the same table at dinner with her? A. I was.

Q. Did you have some conversation with her or just tell us what happened at the dinner table? A. I can't say whether there was any conversation between herself and me, but we talked generally back and forth, a few passengers on the boat did.

Q. What was the appearance of the defendant then, at the table? Was there anything unusual that impressed you? A. Nothing unusual.

Q. Did you see her that evening again? A. I did.

Q. Where? A. I next saw her on the the lower deck, right after dinner. She came down the stairs and spoke to me.

Q. What was the conversation, as near as you can recall? A. Well, she made some pleasant remark about the trip, and I said, yes, it was a nice night for the trip, and she remarked that she was sorry she couldn't enjoy it more, as she had a headache.

Q. Do you recall anything else of that conversation? A. She further said she had had an unhappy life, with some grief, and I laughingly remarked that she had nothing on me or any other human being, as we probably all had our share of grief and trouble but she continued a little further in that direction.

Q. Just tell us what she said. A. Well, she said she had had an unfortunate occurrence with a friend, but not at any time did she say to me—

Mr. Conway: I object to what she didn't say.

The Court: Just what she did say and not what she didn't say.

The Witness: A friend.

Q. Did she ever indicate the sex of the friend? A. She did not, to me. I endeavored to change—

Mr. Conway: I don't like to interrupt but I object to what he endeavored to do.

The Court: Oh no, I will allow that in. Exception to the defendant.

The Witness: I will say I interrupted and I said, "Well, hadn't we better sit down?" There was nobody on the deck, and we were standing at the bottom of the stairs, where I was when she came down the stairs and made some pleasant talk. We went and say down, and during the sitting, she asked me if I believe in the power of one person over another, and I said that was a subject that I had never gone into, but didn't believe much in that stuff. I said I had been asked that question before and I never could quite swallow that stuff. She said she thought there was something to it and having had this unpleasantness in her life, that seemed to grieve her, she was interred. "Well," I laughingly said to her, "Why don't you try Christian Science," to which she promptly replied, "Oh, I have. I have tried Christian Science and I don't like it; I hate it." I said, "How is that? What was your experience?" Her reply was that Christian Science taught its pupils to forgive those who trespassed against them, and she had forgiven the friend who had hurt her and this friend had come back, only to hurt her more than before, and therefore she felt hateful toward Christian Science. Well, we stayed there for a few minutes and I had nothing apparently in common to talk about with the defendant. So I suggested, hadn't we better walk around the deck. In the meantime, nobody had come into the room where we were. It was the general parlor on the lower deck of the boat. She said, yes, she would like to. So we went up those stairs inside the boat and in the room above, in the parlor above, there was a piano. She noticed it and she said, "Oh, here is a piano!" She moved over to one end of the piano to remove the cover, and I went to the other end to help her. We removed the cover and she turned up the top and ran her fingers over the keys and immediately music came out of it. She was musical. I said to her, "Why, play something." She sat down to the piano and played a song, played and sang two songs. At that time, I regarded her voice as one of the most pleasing voices I had ever heard anywhere. I said nothing, sitting there. She arose from the seat and I said, "Go ahead, go ahead; you have a beautiful voice, you have an unusual voice." She said, "No, I can't sing anymore," and with that we went out and walked around the deck two or three times.

From Savannah to New York-Lillian

The two-and-a-half-day trip back to New York was fairly un-eventful. There were twenty some odd people on the *St. Louis*, and I couldn't think past my pounding headache. I engaged a few people in conversation and although I don't remember much, apparently I made a weird impression on them. One hour melted into the next. It seemed like I was docking in New York within minutes. Time was illusive. I met Albert Bradley and he took me to the Breslin Hotel.

TRIAL TRANSCRIPT PAGES 981, 982, 985, 986

Lillian's Testimony

Q. Then what did you do? A. Then I sewed up my scarf.

Q. With the gun? A. Yes.

Q. How did you sew the gun in your scarf? A. I didn't sew the gun to the scarf. I sewed the scarf.

Q. How do you mean, I don't understand it? A. I took the scarf and placed it together and sewed it.

Q. Like a muff? A. Yes.

Q. What did you do with the gun? A. I placed it inside of the scarf.

Q. Did you go out? A. Yes.

Q. How did you carry the gun, in the scarf? A. I carried the gun inside the scarf.

Q. All the way to Brooklyn? A. Yes.

Q. Didn't you have a muff? A. No.

Q. Did you have a scarf for a long time? A. Yes.

Q. Was the gun loaded? A. Yes.

Q. Did you load it? A. Yes.

Q. Where? A. At the hotel.

Q. Saturday morning—Saturday afternoon? A. It was loaded, I carried it loaded in the bag from Jacksonville.

Q. Who loaded it in Jacksonville? A. This fellow put the cartridges in it.

Q. Who, the salesman? A. Yes.

Q. Not the man who went with you. How many cartridges did he put in five? A. Five.

Q. The gun wasn't permanently attached to the scarf was it? A. No.

Q. Just in there. Did you sew it, did you sew the gun to the scarf? A. No.

Q. You just took a few stitches? A. Yes.

Q. And you held it in there like that so the gun really supported the scarf? A. Yes.

Q. And after you did that you went out? A. Yes.

Q. Went downstairs. How did you get to Brooklyn? A. Subway.

Q. What subway did you take? A. Brooklyn subway.

Q. Where did you get off? A. Marcy Avenue.

Q. Marcy and where? A. Marcy Avenue station.

Q. Then you got out and how far was that from Dr. Glickstein's? A. About four or five blocks.

Q. Walk there? A. Yes, I did.

Q. Then you have told me what you did. Will you tell why you shot him? A. I don't know.

Q. You don't know? A. I don't know.

Q. You don't know why you shot him? A. (Nodding no).

Q. Have any grievances against him? A. Yes.

Q. What was it, tell me briefly, just go ahead. A. Well, I had had—I don't know how to explain it.

> **Mr. Reass:** You tell him what you told me. Judge Lewis doesn't want you to go into details and tell the whole story just go on and tell him briefly.

> A. About my marriage?

> **Mr. Reass:** You were intimate with the doctor?

> A. Yes, I was intimate with the doctor and I had—

> **Mr. Reass:** You were quite a girl at the time?

> A. Exactly.

Q. Now tell me about the telephone. A. He telephone to me and in the years that passed that I had not seen him or heard of him, I had busied myself and turned to Christian Science and right before I was married, three weeks before, he called me on the telephone and said "Lillian I have something very important to tell you, stop in some evening on the way home" and I said "I will do that. I will pass your home on my way home so I will stop in and see you" and at that time the thought came to me that through the influence of science at last he had realized what he did to me and to apologize for the wrong, so I said I would call and I was supposed to go to his office on a certain Wednesday evening, and on this Wednesday evening I found I had an appointment with the dressmaker and he says to me—here is what I said to him that I was to stop in that evening and he said "I have been thinking about it all day" so I said to him "I find I have got to go to the dressmakers because the time is drawing near" and he says to me "so you don't love me anymore" and I thought it was a jest and I laughed and I went to the dressmakers that night.

Several days later I stopped on my way home and as I got into his office he said to me "you are looking splendid, come in and sit down" so I went in and sat down and I had never expected him to start to speak to me this way. He said "Lillian, you must not get married, you know," he says, "that I love you and you know you love me, we must run away together" and I said "is this what you called me down at this psychological moment to tell me this and I hoped that you would apologize for the injury you have done me" so he says to me "I cannot help it, I cannot help it, you must" and he grabbed a hold of me and tried to force me to intercourse, so I said; I just laughed and said to myself that I was glad I am not the child I used to be and I says to him I said "do you know that if I were foolish enough to submit to anything at this moment what would be the outcome of such a thing" and he said "of course I do, at least we would have something between us that we would love." And I said to myself that is the person who has been treating our family for so many years, that is the person who influenced my mind when I was young and then at this moment I had forgiven him through Christian Science and everything and at this very moment he should come into my life and start things and I went home and I didn't know what to do, I was terribly disturbed and by morning I was just conscious stricken, I didn't know whether I should marry. Years ago I had intended never to and I didn't know what to do, and I questioned it in my mind and I found I was unable to do anything, I found that my mind wouldn't work for me, it wouldn't work for me with the trouble that I had and there seemed to be something that said to me "you must not marry" and I said maybe I should not marry, and I was so upset I rushed to my Christian Science teacher and told her the whole story, poured out my story to her.

Mr. Reass: Did you make a full statement to her?

A. Yes, sir.

Q. What is her name? A. Mrs. Leffler, and she said that man cannot injure you in the slightest way, he cannot have any influence in your mind at all, and you must never think of such a thing but go right ahead and get married and as far as the consequences, he can never bother you at all but don't say anything to your husband, don't say a word to your husband about anything.

Trial Transcript Pages 452 to 459

Lillian Raizen by Mr. Conway:

Q. Well, you had the address at that time, did you? A. Yes.

Q. Well, now after you started out for his place, do you remember whether you had this fur piece here, which has been received in evidence here as one of the exhibits, People's Exhibit 2? A. I remember my fur piece, Mr. Conway.

Q. And you had the revolver which you had purchased in that fur piece, did you, Mrs. Raizen? You will have to answer, so that we can get the answer on the record, please. A. Yes.

Q. After you started out did you go to Bradley's place? A. No.

Q. Where did you wind up, or where did you reach, Mrs. Raizen? A. I went to Brooklyn.

Q. To Brooklyn? A. I went—

> **The Court:** Oh, talk louder. You can talk louder, if you want to.

The Witness: I went to Brooklyn.

Q. What particular place in Brooklyn did you go to, Mrs. Raizen? A. I went to the Doctor.

Q. What did you have in mind in going there, please? A. Nothing, nothing in particular.

Q. Well, now, you went there and sat down in the waiting room, did you? A. Yes, sir.

Q. What did you think or feel or do when you got into the waiting room, please? A. When I went into the waiting room, I felt—

> **The Court:** If you want the jury to hear your story, you had better talk to them, instead of whining about it.
>
> **Mr. Conway:** May I have the last answer read?
>
> **The Court:** No, sir; there is no occasion for it. The witness is able to talk and does talk, at times, in a pretty strong voice. So there is no occasion for it. If she does not wish to do it, we cannot make her.

Q. Mrs. Raizen, after you got there, or into the waiting room, what about any feeling you had with reference to your size, or what you felt when you went into the waiting room? Will you please do the best you can to answer? A. I felt that I had to stoop my head to get into the door.

Q. Stoop your head to get into the door? A. Yes, I felt that my head was higher than the ceiling, and I had to stoop it.

Q. Now, what happened after that? Will you please tell us in your own way? A. I walked in and I sat down, and I felt that all my head came down all the way from the ceiling to the chair. I had a moment of conscious feeling, and I remember I said, "Oh, what are you going to do? What have you got here?" And with that—with that door opened, and I remember I saw—

Q. Yes. What happened then, please? A. Then my head went up again, up to the ceiling.

Q. Yes. A. I remember I walked in.

Q. Yes. A. And I remember that I said—

Q. What did you say, please? A. I said, "Do you know that I am dying?" I didn't finish saying it. I didn't finish saying—

Q. What happened next? A. I didn't finish saying it. I didn't finish saying it.

Q. Yes. A. I didn't finish saying it. I didn't finish saying—

Q. Well, now, did you hear something? A. Yes, I did.

Q. What did you hear? A. I heard sounds; I heard a sound and the noise was terrible and everything fell from my hands.

Q. Where did you find yourself next? A. I was—

Q. I can't hear you please. A. I was—

The Court: Well, answer the question, please?

The Witness: I was wandering around.

Q. You were wandering where, please? Around the house? Did you leave the house that you remember? A. Yes.

Q. Well, now, some time after that did you telephone to some-body? Some time after that did you telephone to somebody, please? A. Yes.

Q. Do you remember to whom you telephoned? A. I telephoned to everybody.

Q. Well, not can you tell us the name of somebody to whom you did telephone? Tell us the name of somebody, please, to whom you did telephone? A. I telephoned to my father.

Q. Do you remember how many times you did telephone to him? A. A lot of times.

Q. How many times, please? A. A lot of times.

Q. Did you telephone to anybody else, Mrs. Raizen? A. Yes.

Q. To whom was it, please? A. I telephoned—

Q. Did you telephone to Mr. Bradley, that you remember? A. Yes, I telephoned.

Q. After that did your husband meet you that evening? A. Yes.

Q. And after that, on the following Tuesday, do you recall whether it was the following Tuesday or Wednesday, that you were brought down to the District Attorney's office over on Court Street? Do you recall, Mrs. Raizen, please?

The Court: Go right on Mr. Conway.

Mr. Conway: I am trying to, but I cannot do any more than ask the question.

The Court: She refuses to answer that one. Ask another.

Mr. Conway: I except to your Honor's statement that she refused to. I did not hear any refusal.

The Court: Yes, there is an apparent refusal. She has not answered. If you have another question, put it.

Mr. Conway: At any rate, I haven't got the answer. I admit that.

Q. Do you remember being down to the District Attorney's office on the Tuesday or Wednesday of the following week? A. (No Answer)

Q. Do you remember being examined by anybody there or talking with anybody there? A. (No answer).

Q. Do you or did you, at the time when you were in the Doctor's office, realize or understand the nature and quality of the act which you were doing? A. (No answer)

Mr. Conway: No, I would like to have answer to these questions.

The Court: Your lawyer wants you to answer. Why don't you do it?

The Witness: I didn't hear.

The Court: Oh, yes, you did.

Mr. Conway: May I take an exception to that remark of your Honor?

The Court: Certainly, of course. Now answer.

The Witness: I didn't hear them.

Mr. Conway: Now she says she didn't hear those questions. May I repeat them?

The Court: No, I don't think so. You can ask the last one.

Q. In the District Attorney's office after that time, do you remember whether you were examined by any physicians or doctors? A. Yes.

Q. That is, after you had been surrendered or brought to the District Attorney's office? A. Yes.

Q. At the time you were in the doctor's office on the night of December 10th, 1921, did you know the nature and quality of any of the acts which you were doing in that office on that night?

Mr. Gallagher: I object to that. That calls for a conclusion and that is one of the issues that the jury will determine.

The Court: Yes; I think I will exclude the question in that form.

Mr. Conway: All right, sir.

Q. Did you, at that time in the Doctor's office on that evening realize the nature and quality of the act which you had done or were doing?

Mr. Gallagher: I make the same objection.

The Court: I think it is the same question. I exclude it.

Mr. Conway: Exception.

The Court: She had not done any act, according to her. If you believe her, she had not done anything.

Mr. Conway: I think she said—I don't wish to argue with your Honor—I think she came in there and asked him this question, and then she heard a noise.

The Court: Yes, but she hadn't done anything according to her, if you believe that.

Mr. Conway: I appreciate what your Honor says.

Q. On that occasion, in the office there of the Doctor, on December 10th, 1921, did you know the act which you were doing or had done or did, was wrong?

Mr. Gallagher: I make the same objection. That is an issue for the jury.

The Court: Perhaps she will say she did something. I will allow it. She has not said so yet.

Q. Did you know that act which you did there was wrong?

Mr. Conway: May I have it noted on the record that the witness shakes her head negatively.

The Court: No; we don't take shakes on the record.

Q. Will you say yes or no to that question, please? A. No.

By The Court:

Q. What act didn't you know was wrong? What act did you do that you didn't know was wrong? A. (No answer.)

Q. Answer, please. A. (No Answer)

Q. Well, what is it? I didn't hear your answer. What is it? A. I didn't know that—

Q. Go on, what is it? A. I didn't know I had a weapon in my hand.

Q. You told Mr. Conway you took your gun with you, when you went out of the hotel. Why do you say you didn't know you had it with you? A. I hardly recall taking it with me.

Q. Well what did you do that you didn't know was wrong? That is the question I asked you, because you told your lawyer that thing you did, you didn't know was wrong.

Mr. Conway: I think my question was, what acts.

By The Court:

Q. What did you do? What was the thing or things you did, that you didn't know were wrong? A. I heard the report of a cartridge.

Q. Now, answer, please. A. Going there and reporting a cartridge.

Q. Go on and tell us what the things were, or the thing was, whichever it is, that you didn't know was wrong, which you did. A. Going there and reporting a cartridge.

Q. Well, going there and doing what? A. Reporting a cartridge.

Q. What else? A. I don't know anything else.

Q. Going there and reporting a cartridge? Is that what you meant when you answered your lawyer that the thing or things you did, you didn't know were wrong? A. Yes.

The Court: That is what you meant? All right.

Mr. Conway: I think that is all.

Cross-examination by Mr. Gallagher:

Q. Mrs. Raizen, you repeated this story in several places before you came to court, didn't you? A. Yes, sir.

Q. Now, if you keep your voice up, please, we will be through with this in shorter time. Do you remember going to the District Attorney's office on the night of December 13th?

The Court: You had better answer a little more promptly. You will get through much sooner.

A. Yes, sir.

Q. You didn't cry that night at all, did you? A. I don't remember.

Q. Now, you also remember that Dr. Meagher examined you quite frequently in the jail, Raymond Street Jail, don't you? A. Yes, sir.

Q. How many times did he examine you, would you say? A. I don't know, many.

Q. As many at eighteen or nineteen? A. I don't know how many, Mr. Gallagher.

Q. Do you have any trouble with your eyes now, that you are holding your handkerchief in front of your eyes all the time? A. Yes, sir.

Q. Well, did you have any trouble in court before today with your eyes? A. Yes, sir, I have.

Q. Do you remember whether, during all these examinations of Dr. Meagher, that you ever cried once? A. Yes.

Q. How many times did you cry? A. I don't remember.

By The Court:

Q. Well, you are not crying now, are you? Are you crying now? A. Yes, sir.

Q. That is what you call crying, is it? No tears, are there? A. Yes, there are tears.

TRIAL TRANSCRIPT PAGES 491, 492, 497, 499, 500

Lillian Raizen by Mr. Gallagher:

Q. You said in answer to a question that you got mercury tablets to cancel the idea of suicide. A. I got them to cancel the idea, and also the thought came to me, too, that sometimes the effect does not—you know—

Q. You succeeded in cancelling the suicide idea, did you not? A. Temporarily, Mr. Gallagher.

Q. You did up to this minute, didn't you? A. Up to what minute?

Q. Right now. A. Oh, no.

Q. At least, you didn't carry it to fruition, did you? A. I don't understand you, Mr. Gallagher.

Q. All right, I will withdraw. Did you buy the revolver to cancel the idea of killing Dr. Glickstein? A. I bought the revolver also to cancel suicidal tendencies, because I thought the mercury would not have its effect—and also homicidal tendency.

Q. That is, the homicidal tendency to kill was to kill Dr. Glickstein, wasn't it? Is that what you mean? A. The thought was in my mind, yes. Oh!

Q. What was the purpose you had in mind in sewing the revolver up in the muff? A. I don't know.

Q. Was it to deaden the explosion? A. No, it was not to deaden the sound. What do I know about the sound?

Q. Did you ever try to purchase or to get anything that would deaden the sound—a silencer? A. I don't know anything about—I don't—no, I didn't.

Q. Did you ever make any inquiry as to whether you could get such a thing as a silencer? A. Whether I could get a silencer?

Q. For a revolver? A. Or what? Or a revolver?

By the Court:

Q. For a revolver? A. Oh, a silencer for a revolver? No.

By Mr. Gallagher:

Q. You are sure you never made— A. I am sure I never made an inquiry to get a silencer for a weapon.

Q. You say you had an urge to kill Dr. Glickstein? A. Oh, that was such a terrible urge. It was such an unhealthy thought. I never felt so terribly.

Q. You controlled that urge that night, didn't you, when you awaited your turn— A. What? What?

Q. You controlled the urge that you had after you saw Dr. Glickstein open the door? You controlled that and didn't go inside right away? A. I will tell you just how I felt—

Q. Can you answer that yes or no? A. No, I didn't.

Q. He invited you in there, didn't he, when the two girls were in there? Do you remember that? A. Do I remember?

Q. In the consulting room? A. I have heard it so much that I have a faint recollection of the two girls, yes.

Q. Do you remember whether you said no, you wanted to see him alone? A. Yes, I think so. I think so. I think so.

Q. Then, you did control that urge to that extent at least, didn't you? A. No, I didn't. I went there with the sole thought to get back my soul—my mind—over which I thought he had control— possession. He had taken it.

Q. Yes, you told us that before. A. I wanted to ask him for it.

Q. You often saw a large number of patients waiting for Dr. Glickstein? A. Yes.

Q. He had a large practice, you understood, didn't you? A. He had a large number of patients.

Q. You always had a good appreciation of people who were successful in a business way, didn't you? A. Yes, I had an appreciation for people who attained success.

Q. You wanted to attain financial success yourself very badly, didn't you? A. Yes sir, I had great ideas of becoming president of a mercantile company of my own.

Q. Was there any desire in your life that was stronger than that? A. There was a great desire, after my association with the Doctor to be a medical woman and study medicine, and he put that desire into my mind, and I, at that time, neglected auditing and the business—commercial life.

Q. The next stronger desire, would you say, was the desire to become a mother? A. Oh! That was such a strong desire!

Q. And your sterility you attributed to Dr. Glickstein's operation, did you? A. Yes, Mr. Gallagher, yes.

Redirect Examination by Mr. Conway:

Q. You had spoken about having an urge to kill, in answer to one of Mr. Gallagher's questions. A. Oh, spare me! Oh, spare me!

Q. In answer to one of Mr. Gallagher's questions. Will you just tell us what you meant by that and what you did have, please? Will you tell us, please? A. I had a feeling—I had a feeling that I could not control. I had a feeling when I was in the South that he was calling me.

Q. That he was calling you? Yes. Now, I ask you about that— A. I had a feeling—I had a feeling that my mind was not mine, that my soul was not mine, that he was hypnotizing me or trying to, and that I wanted that mind. I had it one time. When I was young I had it.

Q. Was it in connection with that that you say you had the urge to kill? A. Yes, indirectly or directly. I don't know how. (The witness wept).

Q. Did you think that the Doctor could give you back your mind and soul if he wished? A. Yes, he could have done it if he wanted to, if he wanted to. (The witness wept). Why didn't he do it? Then I would not be suffering so much, and he would be here, too.

Q. Did you have the idea that—

The Court: Go right ahead, Mr. Conway.

Mr. Conway: Yes, I am endeavoring to, your Honor.

The Witness: Why didn't he want to do it? (The witness wept).

The Court: Listen, listen.

The Witness: Yes, your honor.

By Mr. Conway:

Q. Did you have the idea on the night that you went to his place of asking him to give you back your mind and soul? A. Yes, sir; yes, I did.

Q. Did you intend, when you went there on that night, December 10th, to ask him to give you back your mind and soul? A. I was in such a condition that he might have done something. I think, that would have helped me. I imagine—I don't know.

Q. When you went there that night? A. Yes, I was obsessed with the idea that he had my mind. I wanted to ask him for it. I had an idea that I could ask him for it and he wouldn't give it to me. I wanted to take it.

By Mr. Conway:

Q. With reference to the continuance of the relations with Dr. Glickstein during this period of three or four years— A. Yes, sir.

Q. What purpose did you have, if any, in continuing those relations? A. I had an idea—I had an idea—I had an idea that— oh—that I would go through—I would go through Purgatory, I would go through anything, if he could restore me, if he could honor the sin and restore me to the position I was in.

Q. By marriage, you mean? A. Yes.

Q. When you telephoned on December 10, 1921, on the evening of that day, after you had been to Dr. Glickstein's home— this is December 10th, 1921. Do you remember or have you any recollection of where the first place was from which you telephoned? A. I have no idea, Mr. Conway.

Q. Do you know whether it was in Brooklyn or Manhattan? A. I don't know. It was after I had taken a train. I don't know where it was.

Q. Do you remember whether it was a telephone booth or a hotel? A. I went to a lot of places. Wherever I saw a telephone I went.

Q. Were they booths? A. I couldn't tell if they were booths or if they were open wires. Wherever I saw a receiver in an office, I talked.

Q. That is all.

Re-cross-examination by Mr. Gallagher:

Q. One question, Mrs. Raizen. Did you get your mind back when you did this act? A. In the condition I was in I thought I did.

Q. You thought you did. Did you think so that same night? A. I thought I did. I thought I did.

Q. What do you think now? A. It was all wrong, Mr. Gallagher, it was all wrong. I might have been cured. Why didn't they cure me? I might have got the thought away from me in some way or other. (The witness wept).

Q. That is all.

    The Witness: Nobody understood me. (The witness wept).

    The Court: Stop, please.

    The Witness: Yes, sir.

By Mr. Conway:

Q. When you had been South, in either Jacksonville or Daytona, were you able to concentrate on anything? A. Mr. Conway—

Q. Just yes or no, please. A. No, sir.

Q. Did you have any feelings of reality, or did things appear to you to be real or unreal? A. Everything seemed unreal to me.

Q. What do you mean? A. Reality—creation seemed unreal.

Q. What do you mean by that? A. Everything seemed unreal, unnatural.

Q. What appeared unnatural, if you can recall? A. Everything. Even myself when I looked at myself. I didn't know myself. When I saw something growing in the ground. I wondered at it. It looked queer to me. Creation itself—humanity. I couldn't understand it all. It all looked funny.

People were moving about doing things, interested, and I couldn't understand.

MURDER (or Pulling the Trigger)

Like Alice, who ate the mushroom, I grew large. So large that I had to slump, so my head wouldn't hit the ceiling. This was how I felt at the moment I entered the doctor's office waiting to go into his exam room. There was no thought; my mind just a blank, waiting. I felt as though *my* demise was imminent. Unaware of the weapon I was holding, the door opened. I saw his face, the face that haunted me wherever I was, the face that was dripping with sweat after he raped me while taking my soul, my very essence, the face that lured me in with flattery and promises, the face of purpose when planning my abortion, the face of no conscience, no morals, no remorse, no culpability, the face of evil. My body jolted by the report of the cartridge. The gun had fired. My life was restored.

It was reported that I dropped my muff and left the office. I do not have recollection of anything that happened until I hit the streets. I walked around aimlessly, unaware of my surroundings. Eventually I called home. I told my father that I thought his friend, Dr. Glickstein, was shot. He couldn't understand what I was trying to tell him. He didn't expect that I would be in Brooklyn, as I didn't tell my family that I was coming home from Florida. He was confused and in disbelief. He asked me exactly where I was, but I didn't know. I called Bradley, my friend, and said the same thing. It wasn't until I called Charles that the events came into focus. I knew I had shot Glickstein with the revolver I purchased in Florida. After giving Charles my location, he and my father came to get me.

TRIAL TRANSCRIPT PAGES 639 TO 642

Harry C. Honeck, 149 Raymond Street, Borough of Brooklyn, called as a witness in behalf of the defendant, being duly sworn, testified as follows:

Direct Examination by Mr. Conway:

Q. Mr. Honeck, you are the warden of the Raymond Street Jail, are you not? A. I am.

Q. And you have charge of the prisoners who are in the Raymond Street Jail, have you not? A. I have.

Q. Do you recall in December, 1921, that the accused, Lillian Raizen was brought to the Raymond Street Jail and lodged there? A. I do.

Q. Did you have occasion, upon her coming there, about December 13, 1921, to observe her condition thereafter? A. I did.

Q. And did you have occasion to observe her condition thereafter? A. I did.

Q. Now, will you tell what you observed about her condition at the time she was brought to the institution, please? A. Well, she was supported into the institution by one of the police officers at the time, accompanied by a woman. I have forgotten whether it was a matron or not. She was in a state of collapse, and I accompanied the matron and her upstairs to the women's prison, where I left her seated for the matron to take her pedigree. I left her there with the woman who came up with her.

Q. Did you see her again that day, Mr. Honeck? A. I did not.

Q. On that day what did you observe with reference to her condition? A. She was in a state of physical collapse, and she had to be supported—almost carried—up the stairs to the women's prison.

Q. Did you have occasion to see her the next day? A. I did.

Q. Did you observe her condition then? A. From what I could see by observation?

Q. Yes that is what I am asking you about. What did you observe then, please, Mr. Honeck? A. She was lying on the cot in her cell, and I noticed that her shoulders were bared, and I suggested that she get in touch with her people and get a nightgown. That was the extent of the conversation the first day.

Q. The next day, of course, you saw her again did you not?

A. I saw her every day.

Q. Taking the first week, please, Mr. Honeck: What did you observe about her condition as far as you could see? By that I mean with reference to her moods or attitudes and her condition generally? A. Well, the day after that—that would be her third day or the second day after her admittance—she was in a very nervous state. She was morose. She was despondent and more or less hysterical. She made an appeal to me—I don't know whether that should go in.

The Court: No, leave the appeal.

By Mr. Conway:

Q. You mean she said something to you? A. She did.

Q. What was that, please?

Mr. Gallagher: I object to that.

The Court: I exclude it.

Mr. Conway: Exception.

By Mr. Conway:

Q. Was she depressed, Mr. Honeck? A. Very much. Very despondent.

Q. Did you notice whether that condition which you saw obtaining upon her entrance continued, and if so, for how long? A. She was very depressed for a period of about three weeks after her admittance. Then she gradually became brighter.

Q. How long did that continue—her getting brighter? A. The total period that she was despondent and morose was practically about five weeks, and then she became fairly natural.

Q. Then how long did that continue? A. For a period of three or four months.

Q. Then what happened, please? A. She had another spell, when she laid up for about two weeks.

Q. What was her condition during that two weeks, as far as you could see? A. Practically the same as when she was admitted.

Q. And that lasted— A. About two weeks.

Q. At the end of that two weeks, did her condition change as far as you could observe? A. She became what you might term normal and got around the prison again, the same as the other women.

Q. How long did that condition then continue? A. For a period of about two months thereafter, and she had a third spell.

Q. How long did that last? A. About one week.

Q. When you say she had a third spell, just what do you mean by that, Mr. Honeck? A. Well, the spells consisted principally in her lying on her cot and refusing to get up, and not eating, and complaining of not being able to sleep, and being in a semi-hysterical state, always wanting to talk, and the reiteration of the same things at all times.

Q. Since the third spell, as you term it, what has her condition been down to now? A. There was been, to my mind, a marked improvement in the girl.

Q. Have you seen any change in weight, Mr. Honeck? A. Yes, I noticed that she had gone to— well, I would say approximately about 115 pounds, and I should judge since that time she has improved to the extent of putting on almost twenty pounds.

Q. When she came in there, Mr. Honeck, and during those two weeks, the first two weeks that she was there, did you notice anything with reference to the condition of her hair or her appearance generally? A. There was an absolute neglect of appearance. She made no attempt to fix herself up whatsoever. She simply laid in this dormant state upon the cot, having no desire to get up at all.

Q. What about her hair? A. Most of the time she had a bandage around her forehead, complaining of severe headaches.

Q. Did you notice anything with reference to her hands or anything she did with her hands? A. She had a very peculiar characteristic, if I might say it. She had the faculty of always twisting her hands, and some of her fingers remained closed when she is doing it.

Q. Did you ever see her doing anything with reference to her knuckles? A. She will push her knuckles into the palm of the hand, but most of it is the twisting.

Q. You say she had these three spells, as you term them? A. Three marked ones.

Q. During each of those she was the same with reference to her appearance and in taking care of and twisting her hands and turning them as you have illustrated? A. During those fits of despondency she did not have the twisting of the hands so much. That was more or less when she was up and around.

Trial Transcript Pages 598 to 599

Dr. Stetzer by Mr. Conway:

Q. When Mrs. Raizen came into the prison, Dr. Stetzer, what did you observe about her condition, please? A. Came in around four o'clock in the afternoon, and she appeared to be in a dazed frame of mind, lacking interest in everything that transpired on or about her; showed no interest in anything.

Q. What else did you observe, Doctor, please? A. Well, she was very nervous; somewhat excited and agitated; restless. She stayed down in the main hall probably five minutes or so, and then was taken up to the female part of the institution.

Q. Did you notice whether she appeared to be—what she was doing with reference to any action of hers, as to crying or weeping or moaning or anything of that kind? A. On the day of admission?

Q. Yes. A. She simply lacked interest in anything that passed by or about her; showed no interest whatever.

Q. Did you see her the next day, Doctor? A. Yes, sir, I did.

Q. What was her condition then? A. She was lying in bed; no interest in anything.

Q. What else did you notice? A. Well, she was crying and nervous; agitated, depressed.

Q. Did that condition continue for some time, Doctor? A. It did; about four or five weeks.

Q. I beg your pardon? A. For four or five weeks.

Q. It continued for four or five weeks? A. Yes, sir.

Q. During that time, did she have any fits of weeping or crying? A. Well, she was continually that way, and complained she couldn't sleep. I had to feed her with bromides and various hypnotics. She didn't eat anything. I was seriously considering tube treating her, and I finally got her to take a light diet of milk and toast.

Q. You say you got her to take a light diet? A. Yes, sir.

Q. Well, now, will you turn to your book there and say whether you prescribed anything for her on the day of admission, or the day after admission.

    The Court: Well, if you know, without looking, you don't need to look.

Q. Do you know, without looking, the exact days on which you did prescribe anything, please? A. December 13th, 14th, 15th; every day, with hardly any intermission—exception, rather; every day, I had to see her and prescribe sedatives and hypnotics, so that she could get some sleep.

Q. What do you call hypnotics? A. Well, like verinol or tryo-nal, sleeping drugs.

Q. After that period of four or five weeks, did you notice any improvement in her, Doctor? A. Not at the time.

Q. Well, did you notice any improvement at any time? A. Well, I did.

Q. When was that? A. I should say, about the latter part of May or June.

Q. You said she continued in the same state as on admission, or about the same state, for about four or five weeks, did you notice any change in her condition? A. Well, she had cleared up somewhat, and then of a sudden she would complain of a feeling of depression coming over her, just as if she was being closed in a tight vise, and that would continue for about two days, and then she would go off into one of her profound de-pressions and imagine she heard—

> **Mr. Gallagher:** I object to this narrative, after the trans-action.
>
> **The Court:** Yes, I am going to exclude this.
>
> **Mr. Gallagher:** And I move to strike it out.
>
> **Mr. Conway:** Exception.

Q. Did you talk to her during this time, please? A. Every day, yes, sir.

Q. During your talks with her, was anything said about sui-cide, please?

Mr. Gallagher: I object.

The Court: I exclude it.

Exception to the defendant.

Q. Did she tell you anything about her physical condition at that time, by reason of which you prescribed?

Mr. Gallagher: I make the same objection.

The Court: Yes; I exclude it.

Exception to the defendant.

Q. Now, did this general condition—I withdraw that question. You say that thereafter, after these four or five weeks, after talking to you or saying anything to you, she would get a fit of depression? A. Yes, sir.

Q. Profound depression. I think you said? A. Yes, sir.

Q. How long did that fit of profound depression continue? A. Well, it would last probably four or five days.

Q. Then what would happen? A. Well, she would be very weak after that; become hysterical crying. And during one of these depressions, I wrote a letter to the warden.

Catherine C. Slevin, 166 North Sixth Street, Borough of Brooklyn, called as a witness on behalf of the defendant, being duly sworn, testifies as follows:

Direct Examination by Mr. Conway:

Q. Mrs. Slevin, what is your position down in the jail? A. Head matron of Raymond Street Jail.

Q. You remember the month of December, 1921, when Mrs. Raizen was brought to the Raymond Street Jail? A. Yes, sir.

Q. Did you see her the following morning after she was brought in? A. Yes, sir.

Q. Did you notice and observe her condition at that time? A. Yes, sir.

Q. Will you describe what her condition was, please? A. Well, she was prostrated and didn't seem to have any strength and she seemed to want to lay in bed all the time: didn't want to talk to anyone; didn't eat anything.

Q. Did you try to talk to her? A. Yes, sir.

Q. Did she eat anything? A. She didn't eat anything that morning; just took a cup of coffee and nothing more.

Q. What else did you notice? A. I noticed she was despondent and cried.

> **Mr. Gallagher:** I object to that, and move to strike it out, as a conclusion.
>
> **The Court:** No, I don't think it is a conclusion. I don't know any other way to tell it, if it has to be told at all.
>
> **Mr. Gallagher:** Well, I don't know what "despondent" means.
>
> **The Court:** My limitations do not permit me to know how it could be done in any other way, so I overrule your objection.

Q. What else did you observe? A. I tried to talk to her. I asked her how she felt that morning, and tried to have a conversation with her.

Q. When you tried, did you have a conversation with her? A. She didn't talk to me. She said "I don't care to talk." I said, "Probably, during the day, you will be able to talk, if you feel like talking."

Q. What else did you observe about her condition or appearance? A. She didn't care to get up and talk; she didn't care to mingle with anybody. She laid in bed all the time.

Q. Was she moody? A. Yes, sir, and cried.

Q. Cried? A. Yes, sir.

Q. For how long a period? A. Well, I would go to her and talk to her, but she wouldn't talk to me, not the first day at all.

Q. For how long a period did this general condition, which you have described, continue? A. Well, for about two weeks, and after that she was a little better for about two months, I think she kept it up, that bad feeling and that hysterical manner.

Q. And then after a few months, what happened? A. Well, she was buoyed up a little bit. We tried to talk to her and encourage her a little.

Q. After two months, what happened to her? A. And she got a little better then.

Q. I understood you to say this condition continued for a couple of weeks? A. Yes, sir, the very worst condition continued for about two weeks, and then she got a little better.

Q. That better condition which you described, how long did that continue? A. In about two months, she seemed to be a little better, in time.

Q. Yes. Now, after that, did she have any period when she went back into this cognition which you have described, which existed immediately after her entrance? Do I make myself clear? You say, for two weeks she was in this condition? A. Yes, sir.

Q. Then in a couple months thereafter, she got better still? A. In about two months, she seemed to be more normal.

Q. After that, was there any other time she went back again?

A. Yes, sir, about six months after that.

THE ALIENISTS

There were four alienists for the defendant and two for the prosecution. All were consummate professionals with outstanding credentials. However, the field of psychology was not scientifically recognized until the late 19th century. In 1879, German scientist, Wilhelm Wundt, founded the first laboratory dedicated exclusively to **psychological** research in Leipzig. When Lillian was born in 1892, psychology was just a fledgling field of interest, merely in existence for thirteen years. When these alienists examined her, some forty years later, one could say that she may have been insane or she may not have been insane, simply by speculation based on flimsy assumptions. The subjectivity in the field itself belies a solid conclusion about the mental make-up of an individual.

Of the two alienists that were hired by the court, Dr. John F.W. Meagher had the most prestigious background. He was a physician for twenty-two years with a specialty in Nervous and Mental Disorders. He had many articles published, some of which later appeared in the *Long Island Medical Journal* and the *NYS Journal of Medicine.*

Dr. Meagher conducted nineteen examinations of Lillian. He uncovered some character traits that included being penurious, wanting to have her own way and by her own admission, considered herself cynical and defiant. She told Meagher that she did not love Glickstein, but respected him for his educational qualifications and success as a physician. She also recounted that Glickstein ruined her, made her sterile and stole her mind. She killed him to get it back.

On the stand Dr. Meagher stated that he felt Lillian was sane at the time of the murder and in fact, was never insane at any time. He based his opinion on one of Lillian's statements during one of his examinations. She told him that murder was wrong, and that is how he came to this conclusion. His diagnosis of a psychopathic personality (a character defect) was the basis for many disorders, many of which were not a diagnosis of insanity.

Dr. Meagher claimed Lillian was insane at the time of the murder, but he believed she knew the quality of her action. Insanity, according to the law states that the individual does not know the quality of the action; that murder is wrong. He went on to state he considered her to be neurotic and hysterical in nature.

Dr. Frank Senior was the second alienist appointed by the County Court. He accompanied Dr. Meagher for all of his examinations of Lillian and concurred with all of his reports. There were visits for which a bill of $10,000 was submitted to the state. This was considered to be a large inflated charge for that time.

There were four alienists hired by the defense; Dr. Kirby, Dr. Pilgrim, Dr. Harris and Dr. Hicks. They conducted eight examinations of Lillian. All observed her exhibiting the following behaviors: chronic weeping, suicidal ideas, moments of despondency, inappropriate laughter and evasiveness during questioning. They diagnosed Lillian as having a constitutional psychopathic personality associated with a mental disorder or psychosis. They stated that this was a fertile field for other disorders such as depression or desires of suicide.

Given all her peculiarities and her desire to kill herself, or the doctor (she believed he possessed her mind and soul and she had to "get it back or take it") and assuming she went to the doctor's house and waited and with all the other subsequent actions leading up to and past the murder—assuming the truth of those facts, all four alienists agreed that Lillian was suffering from a psychosis which included delusions, hallucinations, and suicidal and homicidal ideas; Diagnosis: **INSANE**

Only one of these alienists, Dr. Pilgrim, felt that even though Lillian was insane, she still knew the 'nature and quality' of her actions. The other three felt that she did not know the 'nature and quality' of her actions. This is a pivotal diagnosis in a court of law when defining the term 'temporary insanity'.

Summary of Closing Remarks

Gallagher (in behalf of the people)

Mr. Gallagher stated the proposition that Lillian was never insane and was not insane at the time of the trial. He goes on to discredit the experts brought in for psychological examination, saying they made snap judgements, however there were four experts on behalf of the defendant. Basically, they all concurred.

The subject in question was the attempted renewal of relations between Lillian and the doctor right before her wedding. Gallagher claimed that her reasoning wasn't an issue at the time when her chastity and virginity were violated years before.

Honoring the sin by marrying her wouldn't cover the multiplicity of sins she committed after the initial act. In not remembering exact dates of ongoing trysts and operations, he refutes Lillian's claim that the act (rape) was done at all.

Gallagher describes Lillian to the jury as a person who wanted money and position. The fact that she was moody, dissatisfied and worried are common to most people. "Troubles don't make ourselves lose control."

He claims that Lillian's loved ones would have never permitted her to go down south alone if they didn't feel that she could take care of herself. She had the presence of mind to travel from Titusville to St. Augustine to Daytona, where she met a man who ultimately helped her to buy a gun.

After the murder, the papers painted Glickstein as a terrible man. As a result of this, witnesses from the south were sympathetic in defense of Lillian, according to Gallagher. The fact that she spoke coherently in the days following the murder and she hedged on the question of inquiring about a silencer, added to Lillian's lack of defense. Subsequently sewing the gun into her muff discredits her sincerity. Gallagher believed her to be calculating in her request for a price on a 32 and 38 caliber revolver, with "noiseless attachment".

He asks the jury not to believe the witnesses that came from the south and paints a different scenario right after she killed the doctor, saying that "if her mind was diseased, she would have gloated over the body" and walked out through the waiting room filled with patients and not another door.

Gallagher claims Lillian was a deep designing woman who told 'sob stories' and carried out her desire to kill very effectively.

He told the jury, "You are not to be concerned in determining how good or how bad Glickstein was" and then contradicts himself by describing the doctor as a hard-working person who took care of his family, giving one of his daughters a college education.

Mr. Gallagher ends his closing argument saying the two 'disinterested' alienists, appointed by the court, examined Lillian carefully and went over the case. They both found her to be sane then and always.

Mr. Conway (in behalf of the defendant)

Mr. Conway appeals to the jury seeing this case as a detailed description of a mental disorder originating at a certain time and continuing. He asks the question: "What is the contention of the People here?" Were the heinous acts thrust upon Lillian true or untrue? Is what she alleges to have happened, true or untrue?

Regarding the attempted renewal of relations right before Lillian's wedding, the question is: Why then would the Christian Scientist practitioner be summoned to stand with her during her wedding to help her go through with it? Either you believe this or not. Why was she sent South, by her husband's psychologist, as she was in such a bad mental state? Mr. Conway states that these things were either true or untrue. "If they did happen, then certainly there was enough to upset a woman of this kind of mentality. If they did not happen, then she must have been stark staring mad. Either way, it seems to me, that there is no escape from the conclusion that she was crazy."

Witnesses testified that she was moody, sentimental and had ideas about becoming a great business woman. She was known to have fits of weeping and was reclusive. She didn't dress like other girls, when she certainly had the money to do so. Dr. Meagher stated she was a constitutional inferior, one who cannot cope with things in life; that she was easily upset and highly reactive to situations. She was the perfect target for this attack.

This was a man who lived in the same house with her and knew her from the time she was three years old. It is well known that the family physician "had more control over you, had more of your respect and more of your attention than anyone else who came into the house." He was her father's closest friend.

The fact that she was attacked would be more than enough to upset a normal person. Then there was her viewpoint that the only way she could get back her honor and previous status, was to get this doctor to marry her. This attack had a profound effect on her. As per her statement, she had no sexual gratification from these relations with her doctor. There was nothing sexual about it. "She was going through these acts with the hope that one day the doctor would marry her." The evidence proves this. She told him they could be married in Connecticut and divorce the same day. This would honor the sin that was thrust upon her and reinstate her to her former self; at best an irrational perspective.

The doctor hounded her with phone calls two to three times a day. She kept away from him when she was courted by her husband. The Christian Science church gave her a mental foundation to lean on. She was away from the controlling doctor until right before her wedding. He summoned her to his office. She went there thinking that he wanted to apologize for his actions and wish her good luck. However he tried to ravish her again, but she was able to get away. His trickery had reversed her improved mental state, and she felt that she had no right to marry her childhood sweetheart, Charles. She told her Christian Science practitioner that she was going to kill herself and tried.

Although afraid the doctor would show up at her wedding, she marries with the support of her Christian Science practitioner at her side. The couple honeymoons in Atlantic City. Lillian's moods gave way to telling her new husband about the rape and control this doctor had and still has over her. Charles 'forgives' her and wants the past to remain in the past. Lillian could not rid herself of all that had tortured her for years. She began having hallucinations and became distraught. Charles couldn't cope with Lillian's idea that the doctor had control over her mind and she no longer possessed it.

Upon return from their honeymoon, Lillian agreed to see Charles's psychoanalyst, as she talked of nothing more than committing suicide. Upon recommendation of this doctor, she was sent to Florida where she knew no one. She couldn't eat or sleep and lost fifty pounds from May to November. She had dropped into a deep state of irrational thoughts and depression. While staying at different hotels in the south, she poured out her story to complete strangers and writes letters requesting information on guns. She was alone in a strange place with no one to help her. Her obsessions heightened. All the witnesses from the South said she was 'queer', 'a nut' and 'crazy'.

She knew that if she contacted her husband or her father, they would not allow her to come home. She telegraphs Bradley, a man twenty years her senior whom she had known for years. He worked in a restaurant that Lillian frequented, as her job was nearby. He had always been sympathetic to her woes. She asks him to meet her at the pier and he does. He finds her dejected, wearing a moth-eaten red sweater. Bradley then takes her to the Breslin Hotel where she stays overnight, and her family has no idea that she has returned from her trip down south.

Without reason, she goes to the doctor's house with this revolver seven months after her marriage. Her husband was willing to leave the past and move forward.

She is hysterical on the stand. Sentences have to be pulled from her. "Of course she knew the nature and quality of her act. Every man in an insane asylum who arms himself to kill his keeper knows the nature and quality of his act. The question here, as I see it, is whether this woman, in this condition, and irresponsible, should be acquitted on the grounds of insanity and sent to Matteawan?" (State hospital for the criminally insane)

The alienists testified that she was a potential menace. Lillian knew the nature and quality of her act, but did not know that the act was wrong. "If this man had possession of her body and soul and mind and she could not get them back, and she got it into her head that the only way she could get her mind and soul back was by doing what she did, then it was perfectly logical, according to her delusion, to do it, and it was alright. She was proceeding from that premise; there is no question about that. Given the premise, the rest follows."

"It is your job to decide as to the guilt or innocence of the defendant. You TWELVE MEN are the sole judges of the facts—nobody else."

CLOSING REMARKS – LILLIAN

Yes, I kept that blood-stained rag for five years. This was the blood of youth, of innocence, of gullibility; this was the blood of a rapist. The maroon blotched rag was a daily reminder of my stolen life, a life ruined by a man who was highly regarded, a trusted friend of my father, a healer, a father himself, a dope trafficker and felon, a narcissist and a fiend—a man with no conscience. He flowered me with flattery, promises, and false praise. He prayed upon my weakness to assuage his twisted desires.

My obsessions were manifested in the idea of reclaiming myself. I was a product of the times. I needed to legalize that wrong which was so cruelly thrust upon me. In MY delusional mind, the only way to do this was to convince the doctor to marry me—for one day (then submit for divorce), to honor the sin and restore me to my previous position. That which was forced upon me would be somewhat acceptable having been married. I would reclaim myself. However, my hopes of Dr. Glickstein making things right again resulted in futile efforts. Regaining my former status through a short-lived marriage to him was no longer an option.

This obsession overshadowed my entire existence. Twenty-four hours a day were filled with heartache, yearning, self-deprecation and loss. I couldn't give any part of myself to Charles, my childhood sweetheart and one true love. As an unworthy mate, I was in a state of self-loathing, and with the doctor's persistent calls and manipulation, I felt dazed and hypnotized.

Desperate for relief, I found Wilhelmina Leffler, a Christian Science healer. I revealed my entire story to her, although difficult to do through my hysteria and morbid outlook. I tried to live by the tenets of Christian Science, teaching me to control my own thoughts, to push these wrongs out of my life and not to obsess about the significance of that bloodied rag, a symbol of my lost virginity which was bigger than myself. I couldn't change my thinking to pretend these things never happened. How could I control my mind when HE had it?

At various intervals, during those years between the rape and my marriage to Charles, I walked numbly through life. I felt outside of myself. Although I took up courses at Pace & Pace and studied music, my concentration was put to great tests. I kept returning to my overriding obsessive thought: RIGHT THE

WRONG, RIGHT THE WRONG! At the very least, an apology from that skunk might have mitigated some of his wrongdoing. I thought the opportunity for this was at hand when he commissioned me to his office, shortly before my marriage to Charles. Yes, at the very least I expected a full apology.

I arrived, searching for his remorse, straining to hear a long-awaited admission of his heinous actions. Instead I was met with a barrage of rantings. The flood gates opened once more and my memory transported me to his examination table, legs open wide and the thrust of his manhood taking my being. Thank God I was able to break free this time.

Sometime after marrying Charles, while on my honeymoon, I told him what Glickstein had done, going completely against Mrs. Leffler's instructions. My anguish was too great and overwhelming. My father's so-called close friend had ruined me under the guise of treatment for a woman's problem. Six months of little sleep, extensive weight loss and depression had soon resulted in bizarre circumstances.

On the fringe of a complete mental collapse, I spoke of committing suicide and made attempts to do so. Even though Charles had forgiven me and wanted us to move on from those events of the past, I couldn't, in part, because I didn't feel worthy of his love. I had mood swings, lack of sleep, little to no appetite and was unable to live in the present. When his psychologist, Dr. Samuel Tannenbaum, requested to see me, I went reluctantly. He recommended that I get away for a while. To further complicate things, Mrs. Leffler said that psychology and Christian Science were two different schools of thought, and I would have to choose one or the other. I was so torn, but to appease Charles, I chose to listen to Dr. Tannenbaum. Charles and he decided it was best for me to take a trip and with permission of the family, I soon found myself in Florida.

The walls of the Royal Palms Hotel in Daytona had Glickstein's face on them. I began to hallucinate every day and every night, seeing him, hearing him, ranting about my woes to total strangers on the boat ride down and to those who were guests at the hotel.

I waited intently for the morning papers each day. I became entranced and obsessed about a murder trial in Orlando where, ultimately, the woman was acquitted on the grounds of insanity. I felt that I, too, was insane, becoming despondent, moody and delusional. I was described as 'a nut', 'queer' and 'crazy' by most who testified. There was no help from anyone in Florida. I had already written a letter requesting to purchase a gun with a noiseless attachment. I had the urge to kill, either myself or the doctor: I was desperate for anything to stop my mental torment caused by past events and the hypnotism he laid over me; anything to reclaim my soul.

Albert Bradley was my only friend; an older man three times my age, who worked as a bus boy in a lunch room I often frequented, while working in New York. I decided to return to New York, but did not notify Charles or my family. They would not have accepted my hasty decision to return home, so I asked Albert Bradley to meet me at the dock. The voice in my head was loud and repetitive: RIGHT THE WRONG, RIGHT THE WRONG. RETRIEVE YOUR LIFE, YOUR MORTAL SOUL. HE HAS IT AND IT BELONGS TO YOU.

After years of mental anguish, torment and great suffering, I found myself sidling past people in his waiting room, hunched over, as I felt as tall as the room, and I didn't want my head to touch the ceiling (another delusion). I began knocking on the door to his examination room and finally… I saw his face; the face that haunted me wherever I went; the face that was dripping with sweat after he raped me, taking my soul, my very essence; the face that lured me back with flattery and promises; the face of purpose when planning my abortion; the face of no conscience, no morals, no remorse, no culpability.....the face of pure evil. I only remember saying, "Do you know I am dying?" In that instant, my body jolted at the report of a cartridge. The gun had fired. My life was restored by coming face to face with the only person who could restore it. I SHOT. I KILLED, not having, in that moment, any rational thought. The gun and muff fell to the floor.

I did not think if this was right or wrong. During the unknown act of pulling the trigger, there were no thoughts……

only a blur of actions and then the sensation of a cool evening breeze blowing past my cheeks, when it occurred to me that I was outside zig-zagging through people on the sidewalk.

My life was a living hell from early childhood, when the doctor did those strange things, when the doctor raped me, when he aborted my fetus, when he used his Svengali ways to bring me back again and again. I tried to grasp at a normal life but was unsuccessful. I slowly went insane. Most people confuse intelligence with a sense of being rational, but alas, that is not true. Emotions and intelligence are two different arenas of life. Can one be highly intelligent, think rationally at times, yet be insane, not knowing right from wrong when committing murder? I was living proof as to the answer of that question; YES!

Epilogue

After Lillian's appeal was denied, she went on to serve out the rest of her sentence. She was released from prison in 1938, serving eighteen of her twenty years. My grandmother 'took Lillian in' to help her transition into civilian life. It was odd to me that her brother (my grandfather), did not want to help her. However, being that my grandmother was a true humanitarian, Lillian had the opportunity to spend some time with the family, and my own father, who was thirteen at the time, came to know her. He described her as a genteel woman who, being musically talented, taught him to play the piano.

As incredulous as it may sound, Lillian found work as a nanny. Background checks and vetting would not be nearly as forensic for many years. Later on, she also worked for the Salvation Army, and moved into a small one-room apartment above a tavern on the lower east side of New York. It was a walk-up building and I was told that she lived an extremely frugal life. She used an old-fashioned ice-box well into the 1940s. Her business acumen led her to real estate investments and eventually she was able to acquire and sell a brownstone. When she died in 1971, at the age of seventy-two, her net worth was $250,000. Today's value would be $1,614,158.29.

She visited my father's cousin, Howard Cahill and his wife, several times. Conversations with Marie, Howard's wife, revealed that Lillian was a quiet sweet woman, who loved family and children. She always came with candy in her pockets.

AUTHOR'S NOTES

I was in my thirties when I discovered there was a murderess in my family; a well-hidden secret for so many years. My parents did an excellent job protecting us, albeit there were so many questions that arose in my mind. What would drive my great-aunt to commit the ultimate crime, to take a life, a soul of another? Lillian Raizen was her name. The crime scene was Brooklyn, New York. The year was 1921. To my surprise, there was approximately a thousand-page trial transcript that I just had to get my hands on. My father and uncle were business partners, and when they both retired, the transcript was thrown out.

My curiosity led me to the Brooklyn courts where I spent hours speaking to the head of the Criminal Division and other personnel. No one seemed to know where the elusive archives were located, and all of them seemed to think that the transcript should be on the premises. I was sent to another floor where some ancient entry logs were kept. A reluctant clerk pulled out sixteen ledgers, which were all covered in three inches of dust and grit. After two hours of sifting through information, my eyes became transfixed on the entry bearing the name, Lillian Raizen. Finally, another step closer to finding that transcript! I jotted down the valuable docket number along with other pertinent information to the case and the conviction (written in calligraphy at that time). Now that I had something to go on, my search became more directed. A court historian led me to the library and produced the Appeal to the case; one more step to the illusive transcript.

Three years passed, dead end after dead end. A family member, who was a law student at the time, called me with stunning news. He had found the trial transcript hiding in the New York Bar Association Library. Apparently that is where all the files from Brooklyn ended up after a fire that destroyed the building. Among the thousand pages were black and white photos of the deceased and copies of evidence used in the trial. This was the final piece to add to microfiche retrievals of the newspaper articles that ran for weeks on end. Now, Lillian's horrific story is recounted.

AFTERWORD

My great Aunt, Lillian S. Raizen, committed murder in 1921. She killed the family physician, Abraham Glickstein. She was indicted by a Grand Jury on December 14, 1921, arraigned the same day, and tried on February 17, 1923. Her lawyers entered a plea of insanity, but the jury of 12 men convicted her of 2nd degree murder, issuing a sentence of 20 years to life. After studying this case for decades, interviewing primary sources and examining the details (especially the implications of the law where it pertains to a plea of insanity), I decided to write her story as a retrial. The fictional component is her own voice, explaining her motives and the events which led up to the killing.

Just recently, on April 14, 2022, Robin Schlaff, Director of the Westchester County Office for Women, invited me to address the Domestic Violence Council that she hosts. Robi

Schlaff, as she is called, is an attorney with vast experience in the areas of family law and domestic violence. It was truly an honor to sit in front of this prestigious group, made up of judges, lawyers, psychiatrists, psychologists and department heads, and tell Lillian's story. The connection to the sexual violence that took place 101 years ago is a new term, **Trauma Bonding**. This term is somewhat synonymous to Stockholm syndrome. The real sticking point and one of the deciding factors in Lillian's verdict, was trying to analyze why she continued to have sexual relations with her attacker over the course of a few years. Exploring the psychology behind these ongoing trysts, through Trauma Bonding, unlocks the reasons for her behavior and mental state. Bringing this to the forefront in a court of law, with sexual assault and domestic violence cases, is paramount to the outcome.

In light of the on-going work being done by people like Robi Schlaff and her Office for Women, the 'Me Too' Movement, and new laws for sexual harassment and the exploitation of women, I feel that this trial would have had an entirely different outcome today. As one of the judges (and a member of the Domestic Council) stated, Lillian certainly wasn't tried by a jury of her peers, as her jury was made up of 12 men. If tried today, Lillian's case would have had a completely different outcome, taking all of this into consideration. This was the impetus to tell her story and have her commentary.

Although I've never known Lillian, my aim was to posthumously vindicate her through writing her story as a "Retrial".

Gerri L. Schaffer

*Dr. Glickstein lying in a pool of blood
and Dr. Glickstein's examination room.*

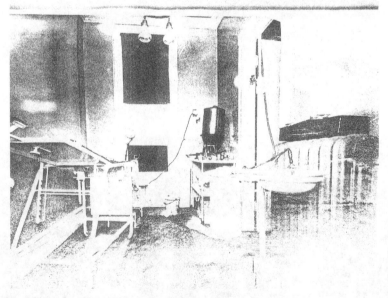

Glickstein Family Gravestone

Glickstein residence as it may have looked 101 years ago

Schaffer Family Residence - 1921

WORDS BY
LILLIAN RAIZEN

MUSIC BY
M. JERRY BERLIN

Valse moderato
Voice

I'm wear- y and blue, Wait-ing for you, You prom-ised you would be

true, You've bro-ken your vow, I'm lone- ly now, Yet my heart keeps

call- ing and call-ing to you, I
CHORUS

loved you when the day be- gun, I'll love you when the day is

done, I loved you when you were my beau, I'll love you when

aged with care and woe, I loved you when my soul was free, I'll

love you be- reft of lib- er ty, I'll love you when I'm free from

bond, To the end of the world and be- yond.

References

Author nk. Published: July 4, 1913. "Arrest Physician After Opium Raid" and "Convict A Drug Dealer". *The New York Times*

Author nk, "What Is Posttraumatic Stress Disorder?" www.psychiatry.org

Health.Harvard.edu 'Phobia'. Dec.2018

Housel, Dr. Rebecca. "What is a Svengali?" www.rebecca-housel.com. 12/21/2014

The Schaffer Tinware MFG. CO. *Schaffer Products*, Brooklyn, N.Y.

The People v. Lillian S. Raizen. 246-445. 41,340 U.S. 1923

Testimony by Sadie Schaffer, "Tr," p. 177

Testimony by Minnie A. Tulipan, "Tr." pp.124-127

Testimony by Lillian S. Raizen, "Tr." pp. 411-426; pp 433-

435; 452-459; 491, 492, 497, 499, 500; 981, 982, 985, 986

Testimony by Emanuel Buchholder, "Tr." pp.93-104

Testimony by Charles S. Raizen, "Tr." pp. 241-249

Testimony by Charles Douglas Robbins. "Tr." pp. 561-571

Testimony by Helen F. Weber. "Tr." pp. 201-239

People's Exhibit 10. "Tr." p. 963

Testimony by Robert Swayne Perry. "Tr." pp.789-791

Testimony by Isaac Cohen. "Tr." pp. 327, 328

Testimony by Lavern Boardwell. "Tr." pp. 779-781

Testimony by Harry C. Honeck. "Tr." pp. 639-642

Testimony by Dr. Stetzer. "Tr." pp. 556, 557, 598, 599

Stipulation as to Exhibits. "Tr." pp.958, 958 (photos)